THE V GA

VLAD

KER DUKEY
K WEBSTER

DEDICATION

To our readers who delight in playing our devious games.
Ker & K

THE V GAMES CAST OF CHARACTERS

(in order of power and influence)

THE FIRST FAMILIES:

VASILIEV FAMILY (V GAMES' HOST—DRUGS/HUMAN TRAFFICKING/ARMS DEALING)

Yuri—Father (52)

Vera—Mother (45) Left them not long after twins were born.

<u>Vlad</u>—Oldest brother (22)

Vika—Twin sister (18)

Viktor—Twin brother (18)

VETROV FAMILY (HUMAN TRAFFICKING/LEGITIMATE REAL ESTATE AND DEVELOPERS)

Yegor—Father (59)

Anna—Mother (45) Deceased.

<u>Veniamin</u> "Ven"—Oldest brother (28)

Niko—Second brother (18) Deceased.

Ruslan—Third brother (17)

VOLKOV FAMILY (OWNERS OF VOLKOV SPIRITS AND OTHER VARIOUS BUSINESSES)

Leonid—Father (55)

Olga—Mother (46)

Diana—Older sister (24)

Irina "Shadow"—Younger sister (18)

<u>Vas</u>—Maid's son (18)

Anton—Diana's bodyguard (51)

Voskoboynikov Family (Oil and Gas)

Iosif—Father (61)
Veronika—Mother (55)
Ivan—Older brother (30)
Artur—Younger brother (28)
Alyona—Youngest sister (19)

The Second Families:

Orlov Family (Huge Drug Runners)

Arkady—Eldest son (28)

Koslov Family (Smaller Arms Dealers)

Stepan—Only son (19) Vlad's new V Games trainee.

Egorov Family

Other Characters:

Oleg—Vlad's arms dealer
Darya—Girl in the basement
Rada—Vasiliev servant
Danill—Vlad's acquirer of women

Vile.
Vicious.
Villainous.
Vasiliev.

PROLOGUE

Vlad

The V Games...

A parent rears their child and molds them as they grow so they may enter the world as someone with the potential to be great. They do this by giving good advice, encouragement, and guidance.

And most of all: love.

Or so I'm told.

When you're a Vasiliev, you don't enter the world with potential to be great, you *are* great. You're better than great. You're the fucking best.

Because Father demands it.

Brilliant. Cunning. Feral yet refined.

Under Father's reign, you learn how to not only play games, but how to win them all. Women, power, money—all at your fingertips if you follow his strict instructions.

Vasiliev men aren't weak.

Vasiliev men bow to no one.

Vasiliev men are kings.

Father's rules, Father's games, Father's world.

And because we share his blood, it's ours too.

"Good luck, brat," I mutter to my brother as I squeeze the back of his neck in an affectionate gesture.

Viktor turns his gaze my way. His amber eyes flicker with anticipation. At eighteen, he's about to enter The V Games. Strong. Intelligent. A masterful player. My brother will win the games and further solidify my family's power in Kazan.

Vasiliev men don't lose.

"Luck is for the weak," he says, an impish grin on his young face. "Luck is for lazy people who don't want to work for what they want." Despite the playfulness in his voice, I can't help but notice just how much he sounds like Father.

Arrogance is a Vasiliev trait that only works well on an old man who's experienced everything.

Arrogance is foolish on a boy barely turned man.

He may be my younger brother, but my instincts are probably more paternal in nature than our father. I want to grab Vik by the shoulders and give him a good hard shake. He needs a dose of reality. The vipers in our world lie in wait, eager to take golden eggs we've worked so hard to create.

"Stay alive," I say, shaking my head. "Deflate your head a little and don't ignore what's right in front of you by thinking you can eliminate everything that sneaks up behind you. Your eyes must be everywhere—inside and outside the arena." I hold out a dagger given to me by my father. "Here. You'll need this."

He takes the dagger from my palm and inspects the crest etched into the blade. Our family crest. The imperial two-headed eagle. When Viktor completes The V Games, another head will be added.

Powerful.

Unwavering.

Brutal.

A trinity of three men who will solidify our family's future, easily ruling an uncontrollable world by using their lust and debauchery against them. A made-up kingdom where there are no literal kings or peasants. A world created by my father to be ruled by his sons.

The Vasiliev men tap into their deepest and darkest cravings. We meet their truest desires by giving them a devil's playground within The V Games. Everything we do is to encourage their darkness. We present it to them like a vial full of heroin waiting to be injected. All they have to do is pull the trigger.

Viktor gives me a nod, his fiery eyes blazing with determination. His arrogance takes a back seat as the adrenaline fuels him forward. The boyish look on his face hardens into the glare of our father.

He will win.

I've trained him just as my father trained me.

Fierce. Deadly. Brutal. Cunning.

Only winning.

We think many, many, many moves ahead.

It's the Vasiliev way.

"Welcome to The V Games," the announcer rumbles through the intercom.

An arena full of spectators roar on the other side of the doors as adrenaline pumps into my veins.

In another twenty-four hours, the same arena will drip with blood, stink of sex, and be littered with corpses.

Stay alive, brother.

When the doors open, the crowd becomes deafening. I watch with clenched teeth as my brother prowls out of safety into the fray. The doors close behind him, sucking my breath along with them.

"He likes to win, Vlad," Vika, my sister and Viktor's twin, purrs as she comes to stand beside me. Her rose perfume suffocates anyone she nears, and I'm not immune. I'm sure it's a power play. She's a woman, and Vasiliev women have a much different role than the men. They're pawns in our game—to be married off to strengthen ties between families we need in our court. I try to hold my breath, but my eyes water from her sickly, flowery stench. It smells like desperation and weakness. She's been shedding her sweet innocence lately in favor of this sly act. I've seen her flirting and enticing the men around us to notice her blossoming.

The problem with Vika is she never had a mother figure, or any woman, to show her the right way to conduct herself, and it appears she's mimicking the roles of our father's whores who've come and gone over the years. It's a game she thinks she's mastered, but she's wrong. Cute and innocent would have served her much better than this desperate act.

"Vasiliev men always do," I tell her calmly, no inflection in my voice despite my desire to offer her comfort in this moment. Affection can be used as a weapon when given to women, especially one as cunning as our dear sister.

"You sound just like Otets." *Father.* She squints her eyes.

I puff my chest in a small show of dominance. "I'll take that as a compliment."

She bristles, and I bite back a smirk. What my sister doesn't realize is she may carry our last name, but she's another viper hungry for a golden egg. Duplicitous and out for herself. I love her, but I'm not stupid. She snuck around with my once best friend, Niko Vetrov, thinking she had the power to determine her own fate. She was born a Vasiliev, so the need for supremacy is in her blood. However, it won't always be so. She will marry and her name will change. My sister doesn't think she's been caught vying for her boyfriend Niko's older brother Veniamin's attention. She wants the next in line—not the second. The more influential sibling. Despite almost destroying my and Niko's friendship in the process. I'm irritated she's made such a mess of things to get her way.

"Where's Niko?" she questions, as if reading my mind, turning her tawny eyes my way. They gleam with satisfaction. Her gaze is desperate to find any signs of my weakness—a way in.

She'll find none.

Father taught me well.

"Perhaps you should call him," I say, a pleasant smile gracing my lips. "He's your boyfriend, not mine."

Her nostrils flare and she crosses her arms over her chest. She wants me to crack. To bite back at her and accuse her of the things we both know she's done. My sister wants to feel in control, but these are *my* games.

I could tell her maybe she should check Viktor's room since that's where he longs to be—just to rile her up. But that would be childish. The way I play is much, much darker.

Niko's affection for my brat isn't subtle, even if he tries for it to be. That's why his and Vika's coupling came as such a shock. Her plans to use Niko to get to Ven are amateur and transparent to everyone—especially me.

She is naïve, however, and has only thought one big move ahead.

And while she may think she's won in the short run, I have every move mapped out until the day she dies. It's part of my duty. Our father insists on it. She is a chess piece to be played when necessary, so we let her have her games for now. She will be marrying Niko. Vika made her bed, and now she will be forced to lie in it.

She doesn't win the end game, though.

Her future is already written, and I'm holding the pen.

CHAPTER ONE

Irina

One week later...

These things are so boring and irritating. A time-sucking waste. My fingers itch to write in my diary—to scribble down all the frustrations simmering inside, just waiting for someone to shake me like a can of pop and watch the explosion of chaos. Instead, ink will display my thoughts written in urgent scrawls as soon as I get home and throw this dress back in my sister's closet where it belongs. Why I must attend these things baffles me. Usually, I'm seen but not heard—ushered away in the shadow of my incredible sister, Diana.

Quite frankly, I'm happy to be there, if I can't be anywhere else.

My brain is going numb, and I'm about to slip into a power nap if this guy keeps talking about how perfect Viktor is—was—and how sad and unjust his early death is…was.

Viktor was as driven and brutal as the rest of the Vasiliev family. His death came as a surprise, but sitting here pretending he died doing something heroic is a stretch.

I actually liked him. Not that he ever noticed me, but he did have this air about him. A hypnotic charm. And it's a shame, at eighteen, he thought he had to prove his worth by entering such a vicious, degrading, sadistic game. What's more shameful is his father allowed him to. Encouraged him to.

The Games are the backbone of all our family empires. It's what keeps us at the top of the food chain. Feed the wealthy their desires and depravities, and they'll keep your wallets fat and your influence far and wide.

My father is a sponsor, and unbeknownst to me, before Viktor's passing, he was also hoping to acquire partnership via marriage. Not his, of course. That's what daughters are bred for.

Bastard.

Slipping a flask from my inside jacket pocket and discreetly uncapping the lid, I bring the bottle to my lips and take a hearty swig. The burn ignites a warm path down my throat and settles in my stomach. An older lady seated beside me on the left eyes me, distaste crinkling her lips into a purse.

Screw you, lady.

This is the second funeral I've been forced to sit through this week. Viktor should have been a sure thing. The Vasilievs *are* the freaking Games for crying out loud. My father let them know how much faith he had in Viktor by dropping a large amount on him competing.

Now, that money's gone. Someone had a hit on Viktor, that much is known, but who ordered it may never be uncovered. God help them if it ever does. It's the rule that no retaliation can come from a death carried out within the arena, but our father, the cunning Leonid Volkov, doesn't play by anyone's rules but his own, and the Vasilievs sure as hell don't either.

He's beyond angry.

And when dear old dad is angry, he gets even. In a few months from now, I bet he'll have a plan to settle the score. I cringe just thinking about what that may be.

The liquor pools in my stomach, urging me to eat something to soak it up.

Drinking is out of character for me, but the rebellious young woman inside me is screaming to be allowed to take over for a while.

I like her.

And once she's out, it's hard to stuff her back inside.

The gentle murmur of the wind rattling the church doors reminds me why I never wear dresses. If not for the alcohol warming my blood, I'd be a popsicle right now. The church is full, but there's an odd emptiness in the atmosphere, causing a shiver to race through me.

My gaze searches for *him*. Vlad Vasiliev. Strong. Formidable. Beautiful. His dark hair is gelled into a style that makes me crave to run my fingers through it and mess it up. The thought of him having messy hair for once in his life has me stifling a highly inappropriate giggle.

Maybe I should calm down with the flask sipping.

I let my eyes fixate on the tick of his jaw. All humor dissipates as I appreciate the muscle in his neck flexing every now and again. I wonder what he tastes like right there. He's sitting to the right, just in front of me. If I lean forward, I could probably smell the shampoo he uses. I bet it's something masculine and expensive.

I straighten my back and clench my thighs. The lady beside me shifts and I notice her watching me as I check Vlad out. Ignoring her barely contained curled lip, I continue my visual sampling. It's not often I get to be this close to him and stare unabashedly.

The suit he's wearing fits over his broad shoulders like a second skin, not a wrinkle or piece of lint to be seen. His polished look is like his armor—it deters people from even approaching him. I certainly never have.

Dominance, money, and supremacy emanate from him in droves, like a forcefield he's conjured up through sheer will.

I've been watching him from the background since I could walk. Learning, deconstructing, and pining despite my brain wishing I didn't. But it's impossible not to. He's my favorite addiction.

I take him in like air to my lungs and breathe.

He appears more angry than sad based on the way he's gritting his teeth and how tense he is. Figures, these assholes are probably more pissed off their Viktor didn't make it out than they are at losing a loved one.

My sister told me a secret the day Viktor died—one that turned my whole life on its head. She was to be promised to Viktor. Father was already in negotiations for their arranged marriage, and she was to be his wife—a widow if The Games had happened half a year later. Another reason why Father was furious. It's almost like he blames Yuri Vasiliev for sacrificing his youngest son to prevent their union.

All my life, my mother promised our lives wouldn't be like hers. That our marriages would be *our* choice and not what benefits the family.

I'd almost believed her too.

When she couldn't produce a son for my father, though, he began to train my sister and me for the family business. Made sure we were fluent in five languages and paid for private schools and tutors to build our knowledge of the world around us. He even went as far as making us travel to be educated in the countries' cultures he thought were important. He reinforced that, just because we're female, it didn't lessen our worth or power when it came to business, not if we didn't want it to.

We wouldn't be bound to make a husband happy while he runs an empire because we'd have our own empire and love. Duty would not rule our destiny.

Lies. Lies. Lies.

My soul deflated the day my sister told me of our father's plan to marry her to Viktor. He was only eighteen, same as me. Diana is twenty-four, and to my astonishment, and disappointment, she was going to go through with it. The words, "It will be good for our family," fell from her lips like cyanide, poisoning the respect and admiration I'd carried for her all my life. She sounded just like Father.

And if he plans for her to be married, then that means I'll be after her and the business we've been learning to take over since we could talk will be merged with the Vasiliev family. It's a good business strategy but it strengthens the Vasiliev's more than anything else. We will be expected to lie on our backs and produce heirs for our husbands like it's the eighteen-hundreds.

I wonder if Diana is sad her betrothed is gone or if she's secretly happy…

Pondering these thoughts, I take another swig, desperate for more of the numbing burn, and run my hand over the black dress gathered in thick layers on my thighs. The material itches and there's a draft running up the back of my legs.

A nudge at my hip causes me to almost spill the liquor in the flask.

I hiss and scrunch my nose at my sister seated to my

right. Her lips turn up in a devious grin, then quickly slip back to two red, plump lines, stoic. Only my sister could look sophisticated with red lipstick at a funeral.

Her hand slides over mine, taking the bottle and screwing the cap on.

Party pooper.

I snatch it back, but my hands are freezing, and I fumble to grasp it, causing it to tumble from my fingers and clatter to the church floor, skittering under the pew in front of me. I cringe internally and begin twisting my earring to calm my nerves.

My sister's eyes expand in horror as Vlad turns around in his seat in front of us. It's almost in slow motion to my galloping heart.

Thud. Thud. Thud.

My breath gets caught in my windpipe as his dark amber orbs flit in my direction. Narrowed. Irritated. Fierce.

Thud. Thud. Thud.

Damn, my head spins as if I've been drinking a thousand-proof liquor and not just eighty.

My lids flutter without permission, and my stomach knots. It's the first time in my entire life he's ever looked directly at me as though he sees me as more than some kid. Eighteen years, and never once has someone impacted me with just a look.

My insides curdle, and my lungs fight for air. I'm paralyzed. If looks could incinerate, I'd be a puff of smoke right now.

His irritation annoys me and excites me all at once. I find my lips moving despite my sister's hand reaching over to squeeze mine in warning.

I want to push him and keep his anger, his eyes, his

attention all on me. To bask in it—to let it soak into my skin so I can remember what it feels like.

"Why wasn't it an open casket?" I want to ask. The curious cat inside me has been wondering since the death announcement. Instead, I appease my sister and father, who would be angry if he knew I'd been drinking and interrupting a funeral of one of the other First Families.

"Sorry," I offer with a stutter and a shrug, but his head has already returned front and center, and my words hit air, dispersing into nothing. My arms wrap around my middle and I shrink into the background, back into Irina—back into the shadow I've always been.

I'm not this rebel—not a woman who could be with a man like him.

I'm just a girl, a Volkov girl, who will do what she's told and live like a bird with an injured wing, wanting so badly to fly away and make her own path, but stuck flightless.

I'm the quiet one. My sister takes the driver's seat while I sit back, unassuming and calculating. A wailing sound draws the attention of most of the guests, and I follow their curiosity to see Vika, Viktor's twin sister, sobbing and clutching onto Veniamin Vetrov. He's holding her up with one arm without even looking down at her folded-up, limp frame molded against him like melting ice cream. She's wearing a pink dress that is almost inappropriate for a club, let alone a church funeral.

Vlad draws my eyes. Again. I want to see his emotion, his empathy for his sister. Instead, he rolls his head over those impressive shoulders, and the tick in his jaw is back.

I take out my notepad from my pocket and let the pencil flit over the paper. My mind clears, and the room closes in until there's nothing but darkness—all except Vlad in front of me.

The calm washes over me as I study his features, the dark tanned skin stretched over his impressive bone structure. Strong jawline. Neat, straight nose. Feathered fans of black lashes sprayed over dark, penetrating orbs. When he pinned me with them moments ago, it was like amber rays swirling around an eclipse. You know you should look away to avoid damage, but it's such a rare sight, you can't help but stare right at it.

I'm blinded by him.

Movement rushes around me, expanding the room and bringing me back to the present. Everyone is leaving. I stand, shoving the pad back in my pocket, and follow the coattails of my sister.

A vise grips my arm, halting my steps. I'm spun around and come face to face with the steel wall of Vlad. He towers over me, but I can't meet his gaze for fear of what he'll see in mine. His scent encompasses me, causing my head to lighten. He smells masculine and expensive, just like I imagined. It's earthy, like rosewood, and warms places I haven't been touched before. The lapels of my jacket are tugged open with the hand that was just wrapped around my bicep, and he shoves my flask into the inside pocket, the back of his hand brushing against my nipple as he does. It's not intentional, but I feel it everywhere. He makes the air around me condense, and my lungs compress.

Breathe, I will myself.

The baritone hum of his voice hits me like a weapon when he says, "We should get lunch tomorrow."

Thud. Thud. Thud.

My mouth drops open as my heart thunders like the cage of a Roman warrior before battle. I don't know what to say, but I don't have to say anything because I hear my sister's lyrical tone.

"Sure, Vlad, I'll have it set up and email you the details."

Dragging my eyes upward, I see he's sidestepped me and is looking and talking to my beautiful sister.

Of course.

Of course he's talking to Diana. Not me.

I shake my head. A laugh bubbles up in my chest, but I gobble it down and leave them to get some air. My childish crush on Vlad has always been a secret, and it will remain just that.

CHAPTER TWO

Vlad

Two Months After the V Games...

"The Vetrovs won't budge," I tell Father, a headache brutalizing me from the inside out. I refrain from rubbing at my temples and drain the rest of the vodka in my tumbler.

Father's brows pull together in his signature scowl. Even at twenty-two, that scowl makes me feel as if I'm nine again and caught kicking a ball in his study when I'm not allowed inside.

Irritated.

Bothered as fuck.

Disappointed.

Yuri Vasiliev, my father, has a way of making you feel as though you're not even trying, despite the fact that you may have done everything. He's taught me well, but one thing I can never escape is the way he makes me feel when he's scowling at me in a mix of disappointment and aggravation.

Knowing my answer won't be good enough, I continue. "Yegor wants the land near the border. He wants the land because we want the land. There's no convincing him," I grit out. "I've spent the better part of three weeks offering him everything under the sun."

But that's a lie.

I haven't offered the thing he wants most.

Father's eyes narrow—the only indication of his mood. He knows what I want. Question is, will he give it to me? One would think he owes it to me after what he did. He sent my brother away. Banished him from our family and faked his death. Untethered him when we needed him most. We were supposed to be three heads, not two. By cutting off what he considered a weak link, he left us frail, considerably so.

Viktor was a valuable asset. And my fucking brother.

He not only annihilated during The V Games, but he was learning so well. With more guidance, he could have been as great as he was being groomed to be.

Now he's gone.

Sent off to America.

Father exposed his own weakness in doing so. An accident. An untraceable murder. Something with my father's messy scribble written all over it. A message to our "kingdom" that not only does he see and know all, but he doesn't tolerate any sort of failing. Being gay is not only a flaw in Father's eyes, but a betrayal.

The Vasiliev men are to marry—the conventional way—into families that strengthen our power. And although Niko was in line to link two powerful families, he was to be married to Vika, not Viktor.

It was a disgrace that couldn't be allowed.

Dusted his little problem under the proverbial rug and moved on. Unbeknownst to his enemies who were told Viktor took a fatal wound at the end of The V Games.

Despite my anger at my father, there's a pang inside my chest.

It's the first fatherly goddamn thing he's done in his entire life.

He spared his son.

"I'll put a squeeze on them. The government officials are in our pocket. I'll go over and beyond the Vetrovs. Yegor will give up that parcel of land one way or another." I lean back in my leather chair and start collecting the papers on my desk, as though we've just settled on a plan.

But we both know that's not the plan.

Father must be getting old and tired because he lets out a heavy sigh—a small signal that I've won. Vika might be Daddy's little girl, but she's very manipulative, and our father cannot stand disobedience or women trying to play games with men.

"Vika will marry a Vetrov," Father grunts, his jaw ticking.

He hates giving in. Hardly ever does. But he, like myself, sees the bigger picture. Always thinking many moves ahead.

"Yegor's too old," I say with a smirk.

Father's nostrils flare, a burst of anger bubbling to the surface. I want to fucking throw my head back and laugh at the hilarity of it all. It would appear Father taught me too well. I can play his goddamn games better than he can.

"Yegor's a fool. I'll not have my daughter—a Vasiliev—marry a man who has to wear his pants below his gluttonous stomach. He has no pride in himself, and I won't have him rutting on my girl like a wild beast during mating season," he seethes, rage overcoming him for a moment. To say Yegor and Father have their disagreements is an understatement. "She is better than that pig."

"Ah, I see." I arch a brow at him. "Well, she certainly

can't marry Niko anymore." Our sister, despite the rules, conspired with her lover via an underhanded move to take out our brother after he was the clear victor of The V Games. Niko, also a player in The Games, lurked until the very last moment to strike. Such an evil move, straight from Vika's playbook. Viktor found an ally, though—a skinny, feisty girl who could bring a grown man to his knees only to cut his throat—and she saved his neck by stabbing Niko when he went for my brother.

But the sting of her treachery impacted me more than anything in my life. With a mother who abandoned us and fled after the twins were born, and a father who ruled with an iron fist, leaving affection to the nannies and servants, the three of us formed a bond stronger than that of normal siblings. We only had each other to rely on, and that exploded the day Vika decided her pride and own agenda was worth more than her brother's life. She sealed her fate that day. She's now my sister only in name.

"Niko was weak, Vlad," Father hisses. "She'll marry Veniamin."

At this, I want to laugh. Veniamin may like to play with his brother's toys, but he doesn't keep them, and he certainly doesn't play with my sister. Never has. He knows what an obnoxious backstabber Vika is. Instead, I throw his words back at him. "He is better than that..." *Pig.* Father's eyes narrow, begging me to say the word so he can roar and rage at me. But since I enjoy poking at him, I simply keep going as if I wasn't about to call our sister a disgusting bitch of a woman. "He is better than that father of his."

Father's lips purse into a line.

"Which is why you need him," I say, sitting up in my chair. I crack my neck to the right, then left.

"Go on," he says, intrigue lacing his tone.

"We both know Vika is vindictive, which is actually an understatement. The moment he pisses her off, Ven will somehow end up with a knife in his back."

Father growls. "What do you suggest we do?"

I grin at him, my smile predatory. "She can marry Ruslan."

"He's a boy and hardly capable of providing for my Vika," he snaps, the vein in his neck throbbing. I don't see my father angry often, but when I do, it's like cocaine rushing through my bloodstream. I'm flying high and crave more.

"Which is exactly why he's perfect for her. Do you think our—" *manipulative evil viper* "—sweet Vika can persuade Ven? He's nearly twice her age and hard. Rus is young, soft, and pliable. He's the in we need."

Father's fury melts away and his calculating expression morphs his features. I'm already missing his loss of control, but I win either way. When he decides on the arrangement of Ruslan and Vika to marry, I'll get the satisfaction of knowing she'll be forced to wed someone unattractive and weak—two things she hates most. And since I despise her for what she has done to our brother, that's music to my fucking ears.

"We'll have to wait until he turns eighteen in a couple months," Father ponders aloud.

I have all the time in the world.

"The engagement doesn't have to wait, though," I urge. "We can have this settled and decided by the end of the week. This time next week, we'll be drunk and fat on a celebratory pig roast as we wish them well on their future marriage." The animal on the fire won't be the only pig getting roasted.

Fuck you, Vika.

You got the only person I truly ever felt close to sent away, and now you'll pay.

"Very well," Father agrees with a sigh. "I'll meet with Yegor and we'll settle this once and for all. Ruslan and Vika's marriage in exchange for his parcel of land. As soon as we have the land, I want it done. We need that opening with Nizhny Novgorod."

"Of course, sir."

He pinches the bridge of his nose. "You'll have to break the news to her. I've got business to attend to." He rises from his chair and stalks from my office without a backwards glance.

Another weakness. He doesn't want to deal with my bratty sister when she has the meltdown of the century. I'm sure he sees our mother's eyes glaring back at him when Vika lets loose. Vika is the only person I've ever seen raise her voice to our father and live to tell the tale.

A smile turns the corners of my lips up. "I'll be glad to tell Vika the exciting news, Father," I utter long after he's gone. I text her to meet me in my office and count down the seconds until she arrives.

The moment I get a whiff of her cloying stench, I glance up to see Vika standing in my doorway in a pristine cream-colored pantsuit. She stares at me with suspicion dancing in eyes identical to our brother's. Her dark brown hair, cut in a trendy style that suits her striking features, has been straightened into smooth, silky locks that glimmer under the overhead light. She purses her blood red lips as she awaits what I have to say. Despite the makeup, hair, and prissy fucking clothes, she is the exact replica of our brother.

Gone is the bouncy little sister she once pretended to be; in her place, stands this possessed, power hungry snake.

A pang of sadness slices through me. For the loss of her as well as Viktor.

I'm not to contact him, seek him out, or reach out in any way. It fucking kills me because I know he's hurting and confused. He'll rise again, but wherever he is, I know he's feeling the pain of the loss of his family.

Viktor would have been better off if Father had just killed him.

Awareness prickles through me.

Father didn't send him away to spare him. It wasn't a fucking weakness. He sent him away to prolong his suffering. It wasn't a pardon—it was a goddamn life sentence.

I straighten my spine and file that epiphany away to dissect for later. For now, I'll enjoy the fruits of my labor.

"Please," I say, motioning to the seat Father recently vacated. "Have a seat."

"I'll stand," she snips.

I push the map on my desk her way. Curious, she steps into my office and inspects it.

"What's this?" she asks, her voice tight.

"Ours," I tell her with a wolfish grin.

She frowns. "It says Vetrov on it."

"Soon, it will say Vasiliev."

"How...?" she trails off, and her eyes expanding. "Veniamin? I'm to be married to Ven?" She beams at me, the expression lighting up her face. My sister is beautiful when she's not plotting evil on her own flesh and blood. Ven would be lucky to have her. That is...until she opened her mouth or spewed her hate.

I stand and fold the map neatly. Precise squares. Slowly.

Just to make her wait. When she huffs, I abandon my task and meet her eyes. "Mrs. Vetrov, just like you wanted."

She can't keep the giddiness from her eyes at my words. Whore. "Your engagement will be a long one."

"What?" she demands. "Why? I want to marry Veniamin now."

I stare at her for a long moment, drinking in her vulnerability before I go in for the kill. When I've had enough waiting, I cluck my tongue. "Oh, Vika," I say, as though it pains me to deliver the news, "not Veniamin. Father wants you to marry Ruslan."

It takes a moment for her to register what I'm saying. The words actually lash out like a ball whip and stun her into stumbling back a few feet. Then, she screeches in horror. "What? That's ridiculous! He's seventeen! Have you seen his face?!"

"Don't be so dramatic," I say in a dry tone. "You're only eighteen yourself. Besides, in another few months, he will be of legal age. Then you both can make lots of Vetrov babies."

"You fucking asshole," she hisses. "You did this. I'm going to speak to Father and he'll—"

"He'll do nothing," I bite out, my own anger brimming to the surface. "He'll do nothing because it's already been decided."

She screams as she charges my desk and slings all my papers onto the floor. Her snooty features have been replaced by a snarled, rage-filled expression. Amber eyes blaze like the devil himself is inside her and ready to wreak havoc. "You won't get away with this," she whispers, her body trembling with anger. "I'll win. You'll see."

I simply smile at her. "We'll see."

With a roar, she storms from the room.

Sitting back down, I open an email to send to Ven. I'll explain that Vika will be marrying Ruslan, and that his father will agree to it upon my father's suggestion. That it will tighten our families' bond if we send the *future Mrs. Vetrov* to live there during their engagement, so the happy couple can have a proper courtship before marriage.

And between the lines, he'll realize he now owes me a huge fucking favor.

I just saved his neck by sacrificing his brother to the hungry wolf that is my sister.

Veniamin Vetrov will make good on that favor. He never lets me down.

My father may think he designed these games—not just The V Games, but every game in life. What he never counted on was for someone to change the rules.

New Rule Number One: You hurt my brother, I fucking hurt you.

CHAPTER THREE

Irina

The walls in Diana's office drive me stir crazy. Why she insists on plastering art deco everywhere is odd to me. I prefer the classic paintings, real art, crafted by hours of an arched spine and hand cramps using oil paints and your mind's eye.

"Shadow," my sister snaps the nickname given to me by our father since before I can remember. Apparently, I've been living in my sister's shadow since I was a toddler.

I look over to her from the armchair she allowed me to drag in here. Her auburn hair is pulled back into a tight bun. Smoky eye shadow and dark red lips decorate her large features. She looks like a film star even at the office. Her silk blouse is tucked neatly into her pencil skirt, showing off her slim figure and curvy hips. I look down at my own clothes and cringe. My checkered shirt has mayonnaise smeared down the front from lunch.

"Shadow?"

"Huh?" I jolt, remembering she called my name.

Fierce blue eyes that match my own pin me. "Irvac is coming in next, so pay attention."

Pay attention? Her words are an insult. I always pay attention. Every detail is captured, logged, and stored away for later use. I noticed she's wearing more makeup than usual and the top two buttons of her blouse are open instead of closed like any other day. The warmth in her cheeks is noticeable, and she keeps checking her cell phone, then crossing and uncrossing her legs.

"Are you sure the numbers are wrong?" she urges.

"Numbers don't lie, Diana," I say in a terse tone. "The people inputting the numbers lie."

She sighs and takes a swig from a cup on her desk. She drinks too much coffee.

"This is unfortunate. Irvac has been with us a long time."

I flit my fingers over my laptop and bring up the spreadsheet to show her the inaccuracy. We have more products leaving our warehouses than the return being entered. It's small in the grand scheme of things, but it's there, and thieves get greedy if left unpunished.

Volkov Spirits is one of the fastest growing companies in Russia with plans to expand our offices to Paris, New York, and London within seven years. Our product is exported in over thirty-five countries so far, and we employ over five thousand people, so our management needs to be loyal and capable.

Our legitimate businesses are the foundation for the other side of our business, and they need to be ran with the same reprimands to avoid these unfortunate events from reoccurring.

A knock at the door alerts us to Irvac's presence. Diana's office is situated in our father's mansion. It shows her supremacy—makes us both less vulnerable to the men in this business who see women as inferior to them. It's a power play, a *my dick is bigger than yours* show of dominance. Look where we live and see the money and influence behind us.

"Come in, Irvac." Diana welcomes him with a hand motion to the chair in front of the enormous mahogany desk she had hand-carved with our family crest and shipped in from Japan. The lone, giant peregrine falcon's wings inside the etched crest span the entire length of the desk. Long and tipped in black. Instead of a curved beak, she has the mouth of a wolf. Snarling and vicious. I love that she is female. Father doesn't know this, but I've studied the markings of the giant birds. The one chosen for our crest is most definitely female. Her size indicates so, and also the fact that she has her claws curled around two eggs in a protective, motherly way. She's fierce and takes shit from no one.

"Ma'am," he greets. He's broad and tall and enters with swift strides, tugging at his jacket before taking a seat.

His thick beard hides half his face, but if he's the one stealing from us, his eyes will tell me everything I need to know.

"Irvac, are you stealing from us?" she outright asks, just like we practiced. It's an old trick used by my father when testing members of his staff. Some would break despite the fact that my father had no proof or cause to ask. It's just random and a sign of the power and fear he holds over people.

Irvac sits up straighter and squints, his gaze darting back and forth between Diana and me. "Of course not."

Standing, I walk over to Diana and lean down to whisper in her ear.

"I fancy mors for dinner," I murmur, and she nods. With a few words that are confusing to others, I indicate Irvac is a thieving liar.

His teeth grind and eyes narrow, wondering what I'm telling her. I move back to my seat in the corner, and she folds her arms.

"I'm going to give you the opportunity to come clean this one time."

He stands and rubs a hand through his black, long hair that ends just above his shoulders. "Miss Volkov," he utters in exasperation. "What is this about?"

I move to her again and tap the buttons on the laptop as if showing her something.

His eyes track me, his cheeks heat, and his shoulders tense. "What is it?" he demands, and I smile politely in his direction.

Diana gestures to the seat he's vacated, but he ignores her and begins pacing the floor.

"You have this one chance," Diana reminds him.

He shakes his head. "I was going to pay it back."

Liar.

"I didn't think it would be noticed and I could put it back before—"

She holds her hand up to stop him. Sweat beads on his forehead and he looks back toward the door.

I press my hand onto her shoulder—another one of our many signals—letting her know I'm leaving to get Anton, our father's most loyal subject, a bodyguard of sorts.

As I pass Irvac, he grabs my arm and jerks me toward him.

"What are you telling her? Is this you always in the corner with your damn laptop?" he sneers, squeezing my arm unbearably tight. I whimper despite myself and try to pull free, but he has height and strength over me.

"Let her go. Now," my sister demands as she chambers the Glock from under her desk, cracking the tense atmosphere with the echo of the metal.

He releases me with a hard shove, and I tumble

22

backward against a tall glass bookcase, hurtling through the glass. It rains down around me like deadly confetti, the shards peppering over my shoulders and the impact robbing me of breath.

A popping sound rings in my ears as Diana pulls the trigger, and the thud as Irvac's heavy form hits the floor makes my heart jump.

"Thieving is one thing, touching one of us is another entirely," she breathes, fury dripping from her every word.

The door bursts open and Vlad stands in the doorway, much to our surprise. Diana hasn't seen him since he took her to lunch after his brother's funeral. I'd wanted to grill her about the date, but bit my tongue. She didn't offer much either.

He looks down at the still-warm body, and then to my sister. Finally, his intense golden-brown eyes flit to me. I fixate on his full lips as he casually asks, "Am I interrupting something?" He arches his brow, his only show of brief amusement.

I gather my wits and pick some of the glass from my clothes. Diana rushes over to me, inspecting my face and neck like a mother hen. Her icy blue eyes flicker with worry. My sister may be a badass most of the time, but sometimes, only to me, she'll show a glimpse of the girl I used to run with through the woods behind our house as we pretended to be evil queens hunting down our lowly peasants. I can almost hear her childhood cackling—

"Are you injured?" she asks, concern pulling her brows down in a scowl as she helps me to my feet. All traces of the smiley, fun-loving sister I grew up with are gone. The serious, shrewd powerhouse of a woman is back in place.

"I'll be fine," I assure her, my voice terse. I step past her, but have to stop when Vlad doesn't move from the doorway, blocking me from fleeing. I look up at him, expecting him to be studying Diana or the scene before him, because I'm invisible to him—to everyone—but our eyes clash, and the world stops moving.

My heart slows, and the blood rushes through my veins like wine into a goblet over dinner. Looking at him up close is like seeing all Seven Wonders of the World at once. Like hearing my favorite song sang live and just for me. Seconds pass, but they feel like hours. His eyes skim from my eyes to my nose. My cheeks heat at his careful inspection. The moment I blush, one corner of his lips twitch as though he might smile. He doesn't. Instead, he continues staring down at me, this time landing on my lips. I part them slightly as if to drink him in.

I can taste his breath.

I can sense the beating of his heart.

I can almost hear his thoughts.

My own heart is whispering, "Recognize me." And just like that, he moves out of my way to take the seat Irvac just vacated and the moment is gone. All the air leaves me in a rush, and I stumble from the office into the arms of Anton, who catches my fall.

"What happened?" he demands, moving me to a seat along the wall of the corridor.

"It's fine," I mutter. "It's been dealt with."

He leaves me to check on Diana, and I gather my strength to stand and go to my room. As I run through the maze of intricate hallways, I try not to think about *him*, but like the dangling of a carrot I can never have, Vlad's perfect eyes are in the forefront of my mind. Seeing me. Noticing every small freckle I desperately try to hide behind my foundation.

I strip my clothes from my clammy body and hiss through the pain of some cuts over my chest. Going to the bathroom, I turn the shower on cold and step beneath its punishing rainfall.

Blood clears to show small slits on my skin. I loosen the braid in my hair and pull the strands apart, letting the water soak through the long blonde locks. Unlike my sister, I have virgin hair, skin, and body. Guys have never been on my radar, apart from the weird allure Vlad has over me. I'm not ugly, just indifferent to beauty. I don't try to emphasize my assets. Makeup is for girly girls. I always have my nose in books and study texts. My sister says I'm more beautiful than she is—more like our mother. I know she only does this to boost my self-esteem. Our mother is beautiful, but she's always lacked a backbone, so she didn't encourage me to have any self-esteem. My father's wandering eyes beat our mother's confidence out of her.

Turning the tap off, I step from the shower, wrap a towel around myself, and wait for Diana to come and dress my wounds. She's predictable, and within five minutes, she's pushing through my bathroom door with a first aid kit.

"Anton is taking care of the mess," she rushes to tell me, placing the cotton swab over my cuts and dabbing. The sting isn't as harsh as anticipated, and I find myself playing with the end of the towel.

"And Vlad?"

She grins up at me, her smile lighting her entire face. "He wants to take me to dinner." Her joy is palpable. I need to be excited for her, but it's hard. Guilt surges through me.

"Do you even like him?" I find the words tumbling from my lips with a harsher tone than intended.

She narrows her eyes and shrugs. "You have eyes, Irina."

And boy, do I ever. Those eyes can't seem to stop looking at him whenever he's near. She winks at me, and my stomach twists.

He's beautiful. Just like you, Diana.

God, their babies will be stunning.

"It's not just about looks," I retort, the bitterness dripping in my tone. "He's moody."

Her smile reaches her eyes and warms my heart. "He would be a great match." She places a Band-Aid over the last cut and rises to her feet. "Father would approve."

"You sound like Vika," I snap, irritated at her answer. "That's all she talks about when we're forced to attend any of the Vasiliev's functions." Vlad's sister is a bitch, plain and simple. Sure, she parades around with a pretty smile, but I've watched her flitting from person to person, whispering lies to whoever will listen.

"Enough, Shadow," she warns, marching into my bedroom.

I follow, fury building in my gut. "You should choose your own match. Who cares what Father approves of?"

She turns abruptly, her eyes ablaze with anger. "Enough, Irina! Life isn't that cut and dry, and you know it. Now, get dressed. Father wants to see that you're okay."

We glare at each other for a long moment.

With a cold smile that unfortunately matches our father's, I spit out, "Enjoy your dinner date with your *match*. Let me know when the wedding is."

She glowers at me, gives a shake to her head, and storms from the room without another word. The moment she's gone, I slam it shut and blink away the stupid tears forming in my eyes.

CHAPTER FOUR

Vlad

The past...

"**W**here do you think they keep the vodka?" Niko asks, a smirk on his face. He's growing a mustache, and it looks so fucking lame. Apparently, his father isn't strict like ours. Father says we must always be clean-cut and presentable because you'll never know who you might run into at a moment's notice.

"All you have to do is ask," I rumble, dragging my gaze from my best friend to the sunroom just off the living room of the Volkov home. Father needed to meet with Mr. Volkov. He insisted Niko and I tag along. Niko has a thing for Diana, so he didn't mind at all. She's seventeen, and Niko is always sporting a boner whenever she's near. As much as he hates it, though, she'll have nothing to do with his fifteen-year-old ass. And she might be into me based on the way she smiles at me all the time, but I know better.

A Vasiliev has a reputation to uphold.

If Father requests I see her, then I will.

He'll keep his options open for as long as he can, though, in case something better comes along. Always calculating three moves ahead, just like he taught Viktor and me in chess.

"I'm going to explore. You coming with?" Niko asks.

I wave him off. "I'm fine right here."

His gaze follows mine to the tiny artist—the girl sitting cross-legged on the floor. Her hair is a wild blonde mess as she paints a picture on a canvas far more detailed and well done than any I've seen hanging on our walls at home. She's young, perhaps Viktor's age, ten or eleven, but she paints like she's been doing it for centuries. It's one of the reasons I enjoy coming with Father to his meetings with the Volkovs.

"It's hard to believe they're sisters," Niko utters. "Diana is so fucking hot, and that little girl looks like she has a different daddy. I bet their mother boned the butler. There's no way they came from—"

"I think I overheard old man Volkov say Diana's in the library," I snap, cutting him off.

He's gone without another word, leaving me to watch from the shadows as the girl paints a sunrise behind a snowcapped mountain. The rays are brilliant and almost an exact replica of the way the sun comes through the window and reflects off her hair.

What do you do with your paintings, little Irina?

As if sensing me, she turns and regards me with a solemn expression. There're glass doors separating us, and I know she can't see my face at this angle with the sun reflecting back at her from the glass. Where Diana is all smiles and wide, bright blue eyes, her younger sister is serious. She stares hard in my direction, as if willing her eyes to see me. I've watched her gaze stray to me every time I enter a room, studying me. For a brief moment, I wonder if she's ever painted me. I narrow my stare, but don't blink. If she can see through the glass, I want her to get a glimpse of the real me—the me I'm allowed to be when not under Father's watchful scrutiny.

Her lips purse and her golden brows furl. I'm seconds from stepping into the sunroom and asking if she'd like to paint me. For some reason, the idea of having my face—not the one I stare at in the mirror each day—on a canvas is inviting.

"Silly girl is always painting," Diana says from behind me, a smile in her voice. It warms me that she cares for her sister. Despite her words, her tone speaks of love and acceptance. I feel the same way over Viktor. In a way, this connects us. Perhaps Diana and I could do well together in our future.

If Father allows it, of course.

Irina's cheeks turn pink, and she turns back to her art. With a stifled sigh, I regard Diana. Today, her hair is smoothed straight, and the auburn catches the overhead light. I make note that her hair doesn't have the same sparkle as her younger sister's.

"I swear," she says, her pink pouty lips twisting into a grin, "you get taller every time I see you." Her fingers grip my bicep through the suit jacket Father always requires me to wear. "Have you been working out?"

Unlike my sister, Diana genuinely wants to know. She doesn't have any ulterior motives. I like Diana. I like her a lot.

"Yeah, I guess. I'm getting ready for The Games. Won't be long."

Her nose crinkles in disgust, but she forces a smile. "Ahhh. The second annual. And you'll be entering?"

I puff my chest with pride. "Father wills it to be so."

Understanding flashes in her icy blue stare. If anyone understands growing up under a powerful man, it's Diana Volkov. "Be careful. Some of us would like to see you make it to the other side."

"Because you like my biceps?" I joke with a sly smile.

"No, the suit. A well-dressed man is a wonderful accessory for a lady." She winks, and with a nod, turns on her heel and disappears into the house. A flash of golden brown hair runs past me, a bright red cape flowing out behind him. The Volkovs' favorite housekeeper's child has always lived here, but he's usually not allowed in the main house when the Volkovs have company. Vas *rushes into the sunroom hollering about being a supervillain. He's only about ten or eleven, the same age as Irina, and a menace. Supervillain fits. And true to form, he sets to terrorizing little Irina almost immediately. She screeches at him when he tugs at the back of her hair.*

"Vas! Go away or I'm telling my father!" She won't, though. If she does, the little toad and his mother wouldn't still be here. And Irina is too kind to tattle knowing it would affect their livelihood.

He grins evilly at her and punches his fist right through her canvas with a, "Hi-ya!," destroying the work of art. I'm already storming in there before I can stop myself. I grab him by the collar of his shirt and yank him to me so we're face to face.

"You ever mess with her again or destroy her paintings and I'll paint the damn wall with your blood," I seethe in a violent whisper. Probably too much, but I want to scare the hell out of him so he leaves Irina alone from now on.

The boy's blue eyes widen in shock, but not fear. Something isn't right in the little tyrant's head. I release him, and he runs off.

"I'm sorry..." I trail off when I notice Irina is no longer in the room. "I'm sorry," I say again to myself.

Present...

I pull under the awning of Myasnoy Dom, a famous Russian five-star restaurant. Diana doesn't say a word, but I can sense her disappointment. When I asked her to dinner, I think she hoped for something a little more than "just business," yet here we are at a neutral ground for the families to dine and negotiate. Bodyguards remain outside, and you check your egos at the door. Weapons are allowed inside, but under no circumstances are they to be used. Ever. Diana lets out a tiny sigh before flashing me her perfected smile—one that doesn't reach her eyes.

"I hear the crab they got in recently is phenomenal," I say before climbing out of the vehicle and handing the valet my keys.

When I round the car, Diana is already stepping out. The Volkov women don't mess around with letting men hold doors for them. I respect that about Diana. Despite being as beautiful as they come, she still holds onto her inner fire. She's an excellent businesswoman, and I've often wondered how she does it. Seeing her holding a gun and one of her men on the floor with a bullet in his forehead was surprising, but not a total shock. The Volkov women are known for having spines of steel—they do what needs to be done when the moment arrives. Their father raised them that way, to prepare them to take over the family business. He needn't have bothered, though. Once she carries my name, I will take over it all and fill her stomach with our own heir.

Father has finally given the order.

I am to begin courting Diana. As if we didn't know this would happen when she was twelve and I was ten. We've always known it was our destiny, which is why I was surprised father was in talks to marry her to Viktor. I don't believe he was as clueless to Viktor's attraction to the opposite sex as he made out to be. His mindset would have been more to marry him off as soon as possible to prevent gossip if it ever became known.

Diana's compliance was a total contrast to the young Diana. When we were kids, she would pop off all the time about marrying whomever she falls in love with. But around the time she hit puberty and became a lady, her views changed. Love isn't something we have the luxury of finding for ourselves. We are raised old school. We have rules and traditions. Diana became all about her duties. She no longer ran off into the woods with her younger sister and my siblings. No, Diana began sitting in with her father during his meetings. With her back straight and chin lifted, she listened carefully and took it all in. I know this because I watched her every move. If I were to wed her one day, I needed to be planning, and the biggest plan was knowing the person I would be matched with—every single detail about her.

Despite her fire, she offers me her elbow—a show of respect to my own family. We may be equals in a sense, both being from powerful First Families, but she doesn't emasculate me by prancing off ahead, and that pleases me. That would be more Vika's style. Diana tilts her head up and flashes warm smiles to all she passes. She's good. Really fucking good. Most people—men and women both—eat out of her palm. It's probably why her father has shifted the business more into her hands. He's always been a little weasel, and it usually comes back to bite him in the ass. With Diana, she earns respect rather than demands it.

"This dress is beautiful on you," I whisper in her ear as we pass through the doors into the ornate restaurant.

She bats her lashes at me and gives me a smile I recognize as a real one. "Thanks, Vlad. You clean up well yourself."

I bite back the chuckle that wants to trickle from my lips. She's never seen me any way but tailored. We approach the hostess stand where a man dressed in all black gives me a simple nod before escorting us over to the corner near the windows. It's the table always reserved for me. Diana stiffens beside me, but doesn't say a word. We pass by her own table that will remain empty tonight. This is about joining two wealthy and powerful families. She knows it as well as I do, and despite her being raised to take over her family's legacy, she will be a Vasiliev. With that title comes respect I'll demand she show me as her man and husband.

The Vasiliev name outranks the Volkov one now and always.

I pull out her chair and make sure she's settled before sitting down. A server quietly arrives with some wine and pops the cork in front of us. Once our glasses are filled, he disappears. This restaurant isn't ordinary. You're served what the chef has prepared. It changes daily. Tonight, according to the chalkboard when we came in, we're indeed having the famous crab.

Diana skims the restaurant. She does so in a curious, innocent way, but I know better. She's assessing which families are dining tonight—a quick peek to see who's negotiating with whom. I did my own check when we arrived. Five families dine tonight, three of which who were stiff and unhappy to see Diana on my arm.

A good match, undeniably, if we've already managed to piss everyone off.

I reach across the table and take her hand, giving it a small squeeze. It's an encouraging one from one long-time friend to another, but to all those around us, it can appear as a lover's touch. It'll solidify the fact that this isn't just a match set forth by our fathers, but one we're both in on as well. A concrete partnership. Unyielding and unbreakable. Most definitely a statement.

"Thank you, lyublyu." *My love.* She exhales a nervous breath.

I tug her hand to my lips and kiss her. "Of course, moy prekrasnyy." *My beautiful.* I pull away and take a drink of my red wine. I prefer vodka, but not on a pre-engagement date. Wine definitely sets the tone. "Your father spoke to you, no?"

She nods as she pushes back her shoulders. Her blue eyes become sharp and intense. Business mode. I admire this about sweet Diana. "Ahhh, he did. It's a new revelation, though. Can we expect a timeline?"

"My father wants it done before the annual V Games."

"Of course," she says politely. "I will begin planning the wedding. Any requests?"

"None." Because I don't. I'm marrying Diana to strengthen our family's position. Nothing more. There are far worse choices than the eldest Volkov. Ruslan, for instance, has been matched to my sister, because I willed it so. Very far worse choices, indeed. He's here tonight with his father and brother, Ven.

"I see. A simple man," she says tightly, drawing my attention back to her. Her tone is abrupt despite the warm smile on her lips. "I'll see to it that the wedding is beautiful and unforgettable. A woman dreams of this moment her entire life." A sad longing twinkles in her eyes for a moment before it's snuffed out. Her lips purse as she studies me. "I have requests, Vlad."

I lift a brow. An interesting development. "Yes?"

"I will keep one of my own men as my main bodyguard if you would like me to stay with your family before the nuptials. You must understand where I'm coming from." There is no malice or accusation in her tone. Simply business. She wants protection by one who will see to her best interest over mine and our family, and she can have it—until

I put that wedding ring on her finger. At that point, she will learn to bend to my will and obey her husband.

I smile at her. "Of course. Anything else?"

"My sister," she whispers, her voice cracking slightly. "You help me make sure she's not used as a pawn. I want her to find happiness and love. The real, organic kind."

I'm shocked at her words. "Irina should marry a Voskoboynikov." And she should. They're up and coming over that of the Vetrov. It is also why I did what I did to make sure Vika continued with the plan to marry one of Niko Vetrov's brothers rather than Ivan Voskoboynikov. I wanted her under my thumb. My arranged marriage would strengthen the Vasiliev name. All that came with Vika was nothing but vengeance on my part.

Images of Irina dance in my mind at the thought of her in a gown being married off to a man she hardly knows. Him taking her to his bed and getting to be the first man to ever touch the delicate skin between her thighs.

"Vlad." Diana shakes her head.

"Yes?"

"Are you okay? You groaned." She arches a dark brow.

I take a sip of my wine and smile. "Sorry, no, I'm fine. I was just thinking what a great match that would be for your sister."

Diana's blue eyes blaze with fire as she pins me with a fierce stare. Being under her furious look has me wanting to tug at my collar so I can breathe better and force her to her knees to learn her place when she's with me. I can see why she runs her business so well. She does so with ferocity. Again, quite admirable. I'm lucky to have her in my court. "She marries whom she pleases, Vlad. There is no negotiation. I want your word on this. You'll let her come live with us and she will have free will."

In this one conversation, Diana has rolled over and shown me her belly. Her sister Irina. Interesting. Her pure, angelic little shadow has often been a soft spot for me too, especially now that she's blossomed into a woman. If Diana is to be my wife, I'll need to make sure I have Irina in check as well. I will have one of my trusted men follow her and gain all the information he can. Diana has never shown me her sister means more to her than simply being blood. The intensity in her stare states they are more than sisters. Best friends, perhaps. Business partners for sure. And if I'm marrying one partner, I need to make sure I pick apart the other. No stone goes unturned. Ever.

Irina is her greatest weakness.

And I can see why.

She has this way about her.

I've been aware of this draw to Irina since I was a young boy. Sure, simply fascination at first. Curiosity. And then, with her age, came an allure so intense, I'd find my mind wandering back to her for hours after seeing her for mere seconds in passing. I always assumed my place would be with Diana, even from a boy, so I'd never shown Irina the impact her simple presence had on me. It isn't in my nature to reveal my weaknesses.

Desire doesn't rule my actions, and control is second nature to me.

Irina is not mine.

I can't have her, so I'll have the next best thing.

I pluck the eight-carat yellow diamond engagement ring from inside my jacket pocket, and once again, take Diana's hand. She allows me to slide the impressive stone onto her slender ring finger. No need for a typical one-knee proposal.

"Miss Volkov," I mutter. "I will protect you always from this moment on as you are to be mine. And if that means extending that protection and your wishes for Irina, then it will be so. You have my word."

Her face breaks into a breathtaking smile that earns some stares of nearby men. Jealousy has no room in my calculating heart, but pride does. I love that they are seeing two powerful families come together with a strong bond. So often, when families join, it's out of pure necessity. They sometimes hate their match.

I don't hate Diana at all.

"You can bear children, yes?" I ask before placing another kiss on her hand and releasing her.

Her nostrils flare, her only sign of irritation. "I'm worth more than a working uterus, sir."

A chuckle erupts from me, and I nod my head. "Oh, I have no doubt about that, fiancée. Just asking the questions my father wants answers to." Lies. We already know the answers because I courted her father, Leonid, more over this engagement than I have her. She's in perfect health and has been forbidden to date. Boys are a distraction her father told her, when in fact he was just keeping her pure. It's hard to believe a woman like Diana wouldn't have been getting her urges seen to. Our work is stressful. Thoughts of her touching herself to relieve the tension skitter in my mind and I lick my lips. I study her slender fingers as she holds her hand up to the light.

She smiles and inspects the ring. "This is beautiful." Her eyes lift to meet mine. "As far as I know, I'm perfectly healthy." An eyebrow arches at me. "I'll be saving myself for the wedding night, so don't get any funny ideas." Ha. She reads minds.

Despite her attempt to make light of the situation, apprehension dances in her eyes. I lower my guard and speak to her, friend to friend, once more.

"I'll be good to you," I vow. "I will never lift a hand or hurt you. I'll be a good husband if you're a good wife." I flash her a rare, impish grin. "And I've been told I'm an excellent lover. If you decide you need to test drive the merchandise, you know where I am."

She lets out a lyrical laugh that once again draws the eyes of many men. "At least I won't be miserable marrying the great Vlad. He's got quite the sense of humor."

We're cut short on our conversation when our meal arrives. The server talks us through each item on our plate and the ingredients. I half listen as I scan the restaurant. My eyes catch a familiar amber pair.

Vika.

Fire and fury blaze in her gaze. She's seated between Ruslan and Ven Vetrov. Ven is in a heated discussion with his father while Ruslan has his arm draped over the back of Vika's chair. She wasn't with them before. Perhaps she was in the restroom. Her tits are spilling out of her bright red dress. She's the opposite of Diana. Diana is class and grace and timeless beauty. A worthy adversary. An even better match. Vika is nothing but a whore. And seeing her under the young twerp's arm causes me to grin.

If looks could kill, Vika would slay me violently with her stare. Ruslan must sense her sudden change because he hugs her to him. His acne is out of control. For as much money as the Vetrov name has, you'd think they'd fix that kid's face. When I glance over at Ven, I'm struck for a moment at how similar he is in appearance to that of his younger brother Niko. Niko and I were close until he started seeing Vika. She fed him whatever bullshit she feeds those around her and he fell for it. Poor bastard fell even harder for her twin's charm.

Thoughts about my brother have the crab and wine reacting bitterly in my stomach. I miss him. Fuck, how I do.

"Is everything okay?" Diana asks. The friend, not the businesswoman.

"In due time," I promise. "In due time." When she's my wife and I can trust her, I'll let her in on Vika and the Vetrov family. Until she wears my last name proudly like she does my ring, I'll keep her in the dark, where she belongs.

She parts her mouth open to speak when a commotion resounds from the kitchen.

Pop! Pop! Pop!

Gunfire.

I rise from my chair, reaching for my piece inside my jacket when Diana stands as well. She hikes up the elegant black dress to her thigh where she has a small Beretta strapped to the inside. Her slender, golden thighs are distracting for a moment, but then I'm stalking for the kitchen with her right behind me. Ven bumps shoulders with me as we try to make it through the door at the same time, our guns drawn and ready to fire.

A strung-out tweaker holds the chef at gunpoint and shuffles from foot to foot as he takes us all in. He's manic—dirty and coated in sweat. He belongs in the gutter—not the finest establishment in Russia.

"I'm here for a goddamned Volkov. I know she's here!" he yells. "Where is Irvac, you motherfucking cunt whore!"

Before I can formulate a response, Diana pushes past Ven and I with her weapon drawn. Her words are icy and cruel as she delivers them without fear. "Your brother was a thieving snake. Don't worry, asshole, you'll see him in hell."

Pop!

With impressive marksmanship, she puts a bullet through his eye. He crumples to the floor and blood bubbles from his blown socket. She killed him. Two murders in one day. Diana Volkov is vicious, just like a Vasiliev.

"No weapons!" a man in a suit roars as he rushes her from behind. The moment he puts his hands on her, my instincts kick in. I made a promise to this woman, and I fucking intend on keeping it.

I grab him by the collar and yank him away from her. My fist connects with his nose with a sickening crunch. Broken. He stumbles away for a moment before charging me. I take another swing at him, but he blocks me and tackles me to the kitchen floor. He's bigger, but I'm more cunning. I slip my hand between us and grab his throat in a violent grip. He hisses, and I easily flip him. With him pinned beneath me gasping for air as his face turns purple, I seek out Diana. Ven has an arm wrapped around her. She gapes at me as though she's surprised I just defended her.

Of course I will. It's my duty now.

She's going to be a Vasiliev, and nobody fucks with a Vasiliev.

"Vlad," a deep, calm voice says behind me. "Release him."

Father.

I squeeze the asshole's throat for a second longer before letting him go and rising to my feet. I straighten my jacket and run a hand over my hair to make sure it's in place before stalking over to Diana and placing a finger beneath her chin to lift her head. Bright blue eyes blink at me. Trust. A flash, but it's there. I give her a slight nod before turning to regard my father.

"He came for the blood of my fiancée," I state, my voice now calm, just like my father's.

His eyes travel to the dead body and he clucks his tongue. "Anyone would do the same."

Nobody offers the information that Diana was the one to make the kill shot. It's none of their goddamn business.

"I didn't realize you'd be dining tonight," I say, a slight edge to my voice. Bodyguards pile in and start cleaning up the mess.

Father gives the closest thing to a smile he can muster. "Some potential sponsors for The Games. We were in the clubhouse upstairs when we were alerted to an altercation."

"It's been dealt with," I say coolly as I straighten my tie. I offer my hand to Diana. She steps out of Ven's hold and takes it. "Now, if you'll excuse me, I need to escort Diana home."

Father nods his approval, and we leave without another word.

CHAPTER FIVE

Irina

Voices from downstairs wake me from my slumber. I pull on my silky robe over my nightgown and rub the sleep from my eyes, checking my watch. It's still early. Diana shouldn't be home so soon, yet I hear her voice amongst others. I hurry to see what the commotion is about. As soon as I make it to Diana's office, I walk into a scene I wish I could walk right back out of. Anton, my father, several of Vlad's men, my sister, and Vlad himself are speaking rapidly and all at once. But what has my heart sinking is Diana and Vlad and their proximity. She's gorgeous as ever in a black evening gown, but over her gown, she wears Vlad's suit jacket as though she belongs to him. My stomach hollows out. The world expands around me, and I almost feel like I'm floating.

I want to ask what's happened, but nobody sees or notices me anyway. Apparently, they were attacked at the restaurant. Diana shot someone, and Vlad protected her.

This is happening.

Breathe.

I catch light of the glistening yellow stone on her finger and an ache like I've never known opens up in my chest and acid pours in.

Breathe.

They're engaged.

This is really happening.

My emotions are irrational, and betrayal cuts deep like a hot knife in butter. I knew it was coming. Diana warned me. But so soon? And seeing it in the flesh is something else entirely. My chest squeezes and I blink back angry, painful tears. He was never mine. I need to remember that.

I move inside the room and along the wall, staying to the shadows. My eyes are on *him*—the one who will wed my sister, crushing my soul with every vow spoken. He'll soon be my brother-in-law. Before long, Diana will trade in her guns and business meetings for a rounded belly and planning for a baby.

Breathe.

As much as I'd love to have a niece or nephew, I didn't expect it to be like this. *This* hurts so bad. I want it to stop—to wake up in my bed and realize this is all a dream.

Vlad steps away from my sister's side to stalk over to the bar in the corner of her office. He pours two fingers worth of vodka into a tumbler and downs it. As soon as it's gone, he pours more. Desperate to see his face, I slink over toward him. My steps go unheard due to all the loud talking over the events that transpired tonight.

As I approach him, his scent fuses with my own, and I allow myself a second for it to wash over me. To bask in it. His body stiffens, as if sensing the company beside him.

"Interesting night," I murmur as I boldly reach past him and take the vodka bottle.

He doesn't show any signs of hearing me. In fact, I think he may be ignoring me. It stings. I need this, though—to just be invisible. Eventually, maybe I'll fade into nothing. I pour more than I should into a tumbler. Before I can fill it to the brim, hot strong fingers curl around mine and the bottle is forcibly plucked from my grip.

"Enough, little Irina."

Little. He said my name.

I jerk my head up to stare at his brutally handsome face. The normally fierce and put-together Vlad Vasiliev is rattled. His amber eyes are the main tell as they blaze with an emotion he's unable to keep hidden behind his normally cool exterior. Typically, not a hair is out of place, but this evening, a lock of dark brown hair hangs over his brow. It gives him a wild, boyish quality that makes my core clench with appreciation. My fingers itch to push it from his face. Instead, I down the entire glass without flinching or tearing my gaze from his.

Some vodka dribbles past my lip and runs onto my chin. It's about to drip from my jaw when he reaches forward with a hooked finger and collects it. His touch electrifies me. He brings the wet finger to his full lips and his pink tongue darts out to lick it from his skin. The room spins and heat floods through me. My panties are soaked and I am horrified wondering if he can smell my blatant arousal for him.

My sister's fiancé.

His gaze darkens as he slides his eyes from my mouth to my throat to my breasts. They're barely concealed in the sheer robe and gown. My nipples harden in response.

"Go to your room," he seethes, a furious edge to his voice. "Go to your room, little Irina. This is unacceptable to wear around men."

Emboldened by the vodka, I glower at him. "You're not my keeper."

He steps closer to me, the heat from his body threatening to ignite my nightgown in flames. "Your sister wears my ring. Everything she cares about, I care about too. Diana will be a Vasiliev, and I'll be goddamned if I let her sister get caught prancing around in her see-through gown with a room full of hungry men." He grits his teeth and narrows his tawny eyes at me. "Now, run back upstairs before you get eaten up by tempting the wrong man."

My anger melts away as I consider his words.

The wrong man?

As in him?

Hope, a stupid feeling, clutches me by the throat. I can't form words. Instead, I drink in his dashing appearance. His tie is loosened imperceptibly so, and his crisp white shirt-sleeves splattered with blood have been rolled to his elbows. He scrubs at his jaw with his palm and his veiny forearm flexes. I'm caught staring at the intricate tattoos I never knew existed along his arms.

"Irina," he growls.

His voice reverberates to my core, and I let out a pained whimper. "Mmm?"

He grips my hips, his fingers biting into my flesh, and turns me around. "People are looking at you. Go to your room."

A laugh bubbles from my lips. "No one looks at me Vlad. I'm a shadow."

He snorts, and it's so unlike him, I turn to make sure it is, in fact, Vlad still behind me.

The intensity in his eyes causes my legs to weaken. "When you're staring at the sun, you can't see a shadow." His voice is low and husky.

I tilt my head to study the movements of his lips. What does that even mean?

"Now run, solntce moyo. Go." *My sun.* I can't breathe.

He urges me to move with a nod of his head. I turn and stumble forward. When I glance back at him, he's already stalking over to the conversation. Diana gives him a soft smile before she speaks to our father again.

He's hers now.

What I felt just now was real. It wasn't a game or a move or anything these men in our world are known for playing. Vlad *notices* me. Too bad his duty will always prevail, which is why he's right back where he wants to be with his arm around my sister and a stoic expression on his face.

A king never falters.

And Vlad Vasiliev is the most regal man I know.

I'm just a distraction.

Solntce moyo.

My sun.

Not a shadow.

Feeling as though it may be my last chance to express myself, I smile at him. Our eyes lock, but he shows no signs of his small slip a few seconds ago. Hard. Edgy. Fierce. All walls are back in place.

My smile falls, and I slink back into the shadows where I belong.

I'm no sun.

But it felt good to shine like one, even if only for a moment.

The voices eventually dull and the house falls silent. I always keep my bedroom door open—an old childhood fear of being trapped alone with the man from an old dream that didn't seem to go away once I hit adulthood. That's how I heard the commotion earlier, but tonight, it's closed. I didn't want Diana or our parents to hear me crying my sorrows into my pillow.

How does one grieve over something they never had?

I'm not sure, but I'm most certainly grieving. My heart physically aches. Our mother married our father, but there was never love. Not like the storybooks we would sneak and read. Diana would let me curl up beside her in her bed as she'd read adventurous stories about princesses who were brave and still got the handsome prince in the end. Deep down, I always thought Diana and I could be strong and find love. Why couldn't we have both?

Our world is no storybook, though.

Villains prowl the night—it's most certainly more nightmare than fairytale.

We're teased with someone we could love, and then it's taken away. We're forced to follow rules that leech the happiness straight from our marrow.

I must accept there are no happy endings for Volkov girls.

There's a slight tap on the door, pulling me from my inner thoughts, and my sister calls through the wood separating us. "Irina, are you awake?"

I stay quiet and still, hoping she'll go away.

No such luck.

The door handle twists, and she pushes it open, taking a step inside my room.

"Shadow?"

I hold my breath and hear her sigh before she leaves, closing the door behind her. I inhale to fill my starved lungs, then lean over to flick the lamp on. I let out a startled squeak when I see Diana sitting in the chair in the corner of the room staring back at me. It's odd to see her in the corner, but she doesn't look like a shadow. She commands the space. My sister owns it.

Just like she owns my future.

I swallow down the pain and meet her sad stare.

"I've known you your whole life, Irina," she says heavily, her dark brows furrowed. It reminds me of when we were kids and she'd worry over me. So motherly and loving. "I know when you're sleeping and when you're not."

Nerves dance in my gut like there's a parade happening inside me. "I'm tired, Diana," I croak, feelings of betrayal rattling my voice. "What do you want?"

She stands, and I scoot into a sitting position, dipping my eyes so I don't have to look directly at her.

"I know you don't approve of my choices."

I huff out a disheartened laugh. "It's not your choice. That's the point."

"Father wouldn't force me into this, Irina, so it *is* a choice, and I've made the right one for us both." Her voice is firm and unyielding. It infuriates me that she's behaving like *them*. Like our mother. Rolling over and letting the men in our world control our future.

My head snaps up to meet her blue eyes. "What does that mean?"

Sitting on the bed in front of me, she takes my hands and smiles. "You will move with me to the Vasiliev's estate. No marital arrangements for you will be made. You will make your own choices when you're ready for those things." She's smiling at me like I'm a prisoner and she's just offered me my freedom. But she's wrong. I have no plans to bend to the will of our father, or any man who thinks my inheritance and last name would be good business for him. I can't move to the Vasiliev home with her. To be around Vlad constantly, be around his things, his scent. Watch them bond and fall in love? See him touch her in ways I want him to touch me? Yeah, right. That's torture. *Cruel* torture. I wish I'd had the courage to tell her how I felt about Vlad when we were younger so this wouldn't be happening now. She wouldn't hurt me like this if she knew she was doing it.

"Do you love him?" I find myself asking, even though I know she doesn't. Not yet anyway.

The corner of her lips pull up and she lifts a shoulder in a shrug. "I will learn to." She reaches forward and begins to tickle me, causing me to thrash and screech in surrender. She hasn't been this playful since we were little, and it's refreshing. It reminds me that our sisterhood is everything.

Maybe if she can learn, I can learn too.

I'll learn how *not* love him.

"If he keeps kissing me like he did tonight, it may be sooner rather than later," she admits with a giggle, tugging me back on the bed and collapsing next to me on my pillow. We both stare up at the ceiling, breathing a little heavy from the exertion. Her words play around in my mind.

He kissed her.

They kissed.

My heart rate quickens just imagining what his lips would feel like pressed against mine. Silky. Wet. Dominating.

"What was it like?" I ask. Not wanting to know, but desperate to.

The amusement evaporates and silence falls. I swear I can hear my own heartbeat thundering in my chest.

"Soft, but strong," she murmurs, placing the pads of her fingertips over her lips. "Passionate and intense." She sits up and leans over me. "Like this." She bends and places her lips to mine, pushing hard, and all I can think is they *do* taste of Vlad.

She pulls back and grins. "But with tongue," she jests, flicking her tongue out to lick the tip of my nose. I screech, and she begins to attack my face, licking my cheek and forehead.

This is the sister I've loved and missed.

Lately, she's been one of them, but right now...right now, she's just Diana.

"Stop it! Stop it!" I cry out, laughing.

She pins my arms so I can't stop her, and when she eventually ceases her attack, she looks down at me, her brows tugging down and eyes focused and serious. "I'll always be your big sister," she vows. "I'll always do right by you. I promise, this marriage doesn't change us."

I want her words to be true so deeply, but my own heart is wilting, and she doesn't see that I'm dying inside. Being around him will be brutal.

But being around my sister?

Definitely worth the pain.

"Okay, I'll come with you," I whisper.

She beams her megawatt smile at me and jumps up from the bed. "Get some sleep, little shadow. We have a big task ahead of us."

Yes, we do.

CHAPTER SIX

Vlad

Tonight was a mess. First, the idiot at the restaurant who caused all kinds of honor codes to be broken, then I had to take Diana home only to find myself in a situation with Irina that tested my limits.

Her nightgown barely covered her, and she was so unaware of her own beauty on display for all to see. It was infuriating and tempting. Way too goddamn tempting. I've never struggled to keep my guard up before—to keep my indifference forced on my features.

She can't know she affects me in any way.

No one can.

Diana especially can't know I desire her sister in ways I may never desire her. It would only cause strife. She can't know that, to me, *she's* the shadow. And although she's my match, her little sister will always hold something I will never give to her or any other.

Solntce moyo...how brightly you shine.

When she finally left to go back to her room, I discreetly adjusted myself and took my rightful place next to Diana. Then, when the opportunity arose, I dragged her away from her father and made my excuses to leave.

Now, I'm standing here with images of Irina plaguing me as I look at Diana's full lips. They're so much like her sister's, only they turn down slightly where Irina's turn up. This…this right here, can't happen. Comparing them and thinking about Irina when I look at Diana. Thinking of the way the swell of her tits heaved in rhythmic pounds to my own heartbeat when we were so close.

Dammit.

Reaching my hands up to cup Diana's face, I crash my lips to hers. Hard, deep, brutal. I part her lips with a swipe of my tongue. She tastes of the red wine she's been drinking and it's nice. Her lips move against mine with ease. I'm most certainly not her first kiss.

She's definitely not mine.

When I pull away, her eyes are glassy, and for once, she's not so put together. Her lips are swollen, and her red lipstick is slightly smeared around her mouth.

"Goodnight, fiancée," I utter, testing the word.

"Goodnight," she mumbles, then pales when her father and his number two, Anton, come walking toward us. They may have seen our little show, but she's rightfully mine now. I wasn't groping her like two teenagers at prom. I reach for her hand and give it a reassuring squeeze.

Then, I take my leave.

When I arrive home, the house is quiet. A twinge tightens my stomach when I pass the game room and Viktor's laughter doesn't trickle out through the doors. It's been two months now, but missing him hasn't gotten easier. My feet falter when I reach the kitchen and find the servant placing a sandwich in front of Veniamin Vetrov.

Why the hell is he here?

My interest is piqued as I open the fridge and pull out two bottles of beer. I'm not usually a beer drinker, but with Ven, I don't feel the need for pretenses. He and I go way back. I can relax a little and just be me—the me underneath the power suit.

"Hungry?" I raise a brow and hand him a bottle.

Ven can be intimidating to most. He has the Vetrov wildness about him. Bearded and seemingly unkempt. Barely contained beneath an expensive Armani suit and twelve-hundred-dollar Italian leather shoes. I remember teenage Ven, when we were younger, running through the woods in the snow. Older and fiercer than any of the other boys, including myself. Ven was the only stupid one to run through the snow without a shirt on. As if that made him more of a badass. Back then, he was virtually hairless like the rest of us. Now, his beard and unruly hair match that wild kid I remember. His father may force him into a suit and instill manners on him, but Ven is still the ruthless vulture his family crest states.

He takes it with an impish grin, his tattooed fingers curling around the neck of the bottle. It makes me wonder what old man Vetrov thinks about his eldest son's tattoos. My own father hates mine, which is why I try to keep them hidden beneath my suit. Ven wears his on display for all to see. "Didn't get to finish my dinner."

Ahhh, of course not.

Diana's little murder ruined more than just my night it would appear.

"How is she?" He's referring to Diana. Like myself, he's known her since we were children, and if I remember correctly, used to tease Niko about his crush on her.

"She's fine. Resilient and deadly as you know."

There's fondness in his eyes as I speak of Diana, and I know it's reflected back from mine.

"Ty khochesh' yest', Mr. Vasiliev?" the servant girl asks, looking up at me with doe eyes. She's a much better fit than the girl she replaced who apparently had an accident in this very room.

"No, I don't want to eat. You're dismissed."

We watch her scurry off before Ven nods his head in approval.

"Do you think they're real?" I know he's talking about the girl's tits without him elaborating. They're unusually large on a frame that small.

"I doubt she could afford the boob job," I offer.

He appears to ponder that thought. "Maybe you bought them for her," he muses aloud. "I saw the way Rada looked at you." He grins as he takes a swig from the bottle of beer. Of course he knows her name. Ven seems to know everyone's name. It's admittedly something he's much better at than me. *People.*

"Paying *the servants* for pleasures was always Niko's style, not mine," I jab, refusing to say her name, showing him I don't think their names are worth knowing at all.

He laughs, loud and honest. "He was notorious for chasing the help away. Once, I caught him with his cock between the mattress and base of his bed, rutting away. He'd even paid Ursula, our fifty-year old cook, to shove a carrot up his ass."

I almost choke on that visual.

He just shakes his head. "It's the truth. He was seventeen. Our mother, God rest her soul, would have shot that woman dead if she ever lived long enough to find out about that, and I dread to think what our father would have done had that information made it back to him."

"A carrot?" I snort.

"Put me off eating at home, I can tell you that," he adds, finishing off the sandwich. "I miss him."

I nod my head. "As do I, moy drug." *My friend.*

"How is Vika settling in?" I say with a smirk, earning a glare from him.

"I thought with Niko's unfortunate passing, we were free of that woman," he grunts.

"At least it's not your back the knife will be placed."

He swallows the dregs of his bottle before setting it down with a clink against the granite countertop. "This is true. I must admit, I thought that might be put forward as an option. Me marrying your little sister. And no disrespect to you, Vlad, but man to man, friend to friend, I'd rather marry a peasant than that woman."

"No offense taken." I lift a brow at him. "But you owe me one."

His dark brows furl together and he nods. I love the feeling of having power over someone. And owed favors are my favorite.

"You should still keep a keen eye on her," I tell him. "She's cunning and usually gets what she wants. She's had designs on you for a while."

"I'm well aware of what she's capable of," he grumbles. "Don't you worry about that."

His tone implies there's more to what he means.

Does he know what Vika did?

I study him as he rises to his feet. "I'll be off then."

"So soon?" I taunt and walk from the kitchen, knowing he will follow me.

He always does.

When you know a man as long as I have, you have them figured out completely. And Veniamin Vetrov is no different. I've been studying him since I was a runt and knew I wanted to grow up to be a badass like him…but better.

Taking the stairs two at a time, I smile when I hear his footfalls behind me. Together, we walk down the corridor in the north wing to one of our many spare bedrooms and I twist the handle. I quickly check my watch and my blood rushes straight to my cock when I hear the shower hissing from the en-suite. The servant girl, or Rada, as Ven so kindly reminded me, uses this shower every night at the same time, just after her shift. The servants' quarters are not quite to her standards it would appear. She doesn't know I know her tricks, but this place has cameras at every turn.

There's not a corner I can't see in.

My eyes are everywhere.

Ven knows this game. It's one we've played before. He pats my shoulder and whispers,

"One for old time's sake."

I move across the room and sit on the plush loveseat next to the bed. Ven dips into the shadows and we wait. Patient, like the predators we are.

Eventually, the door opens, and there she is, her huge tits and tiny body confined in a barely-there towel. Her dark hair is wet and clings to her skin. She spots me almost instantly just like I planned for her to.

"Mr. Vasiliev," she breathes, clutching the fabric.

"Come closer," I order, and she doesn't question the instruction. Her legs comply as she moves toward me, stopping at my feet.

"Do you want to play a game, malyshka?" *Little girl.* I

arch a brow at her.

Her breathing increases, and those real tits begin moving at rapid speed. She opens her towel and drops it to the floor.

I'll take that as a yes.

I nod and get to my feet. Ven moves from the darkness, like he was bred from it, and stalks silently toward her. She's unaware, her eyes fixated on me.

"Do you like games, malyshka?" I murmur, leaning down into her space so my breath can disperse over her fevered flesh. Her skin blossoms with tiny goosebumps as her bottom lip trembles with need.

"Da," she confirms. *Yes.* Good, so do I.

Ven's hands come around her neck from behind, pulling her body flush with his. She panics and reaches for his hands, but I stop her, taking hers in my grasp.

"Don't fight, Rada."

"It's better when they do," Ven growls.

She begins to thrash her legs back, trying to kick him to no avail. Her eyes gloss over and her skin blushes a beautiful deep red. I nod to Ven, and he releases her neck, but wraps an arm around her waist to keep her upright. She inhales at the air, thirsty for it.

"Ublyudok!" *Bastard.* Her voice is raspy from being choked.

Ven chuckles. "I've been called worse."

"Feel it?" I question, placing a palm to her heart. Her eyes water and she looks up at me, wounded. "The air sucking into your lungs? The blood rushing through your veins, feeding your heart? To linger on the cusp is ecstasy. A gift. Chase the pleasure, maylshka."

Ven's hands once again wrap nearly around her neck,

and this time, she doesn't fight it. Her nipples are hard and desperate for relief, and without dipping my fingers inside her, I know her pussy will be dripping with her juices. Her lips, swollen and throbbing, beg to be filled up and fucked raw. The veins in her eyes almost ripple as she fights to keep them wide open, staring into mine.

He takes her a little farther, causing her body to twitch and her skin to blossom with shades of purple. When he releases her, she chokes, coughing and sputtering.

She's ready.

I grip her under her armpits, lifting and tossing her to the bed. Her body lands with a soft thud. Pillows fall to the floor as she skitters over the satin sheets. I prowl around the edge of the bed while Ven strips his shirt from his torso. The ink on his skin comes alive with his movements. She's panting, and her body is trembling before he's even neared her. Parting her legs, she invites him between them, but her eyes are glued to my movements. She gasps when he releases his cock from the zipper of his slacks. Veniamin, like myself, doesn't disappoint in that department.

"Turn over," he demands with a growl.

Complying, she moves to her hands and knees. Her ass is in the air and her heavy tits pull her chest toward the mattress. He enters her hard and brutal, slapping her ass as he does. She screams, then whimpers. Gripping a handful of her dripping wet hair, he tugs her head back, making her gasp. Loosening my tie, I slide it free from my collar and approach the bed. Her eyes track me and lower to my slacks. She wants to be full of cock. Kneeling on the bed in front of her, I grip her jaw and nod at Ven to slow his pounding so I can stuff my tie in her mouth.

In, in, in it goes until she gags.

Her eyes water and panic briefly flashes in them.

She moans something around the fabric, but her words don't matter. I pinch her nose between my forefinger and thumb, cutting off her oxygen supply. Ven's hips grind into her while his hand snakes beneath to pinch and slap at her clit. When tears well and then fall down her cheeks, I get closer to her face to watch them leak free. Her eyelids flutter and lips begin to change color. Slightly blue at first, and then darker with each passing second. Her body is giving way to the burning in her lungs. Her starved brain is making her eyes droop with exhaustion. Ven's thrusts gain momentum as I pluck a piece of the fabric of the tie and slowly pull it out to match each forward jolt of his hips. She gulps and sputters with each inch I tug free. When it's completely out, she screams her orgasm while still trying to replenish her body with air.

My own cock twitches in my slacks, eager for attention, but I ignore it for now.

I love the color of her lips.

Blue. Blue. So blue.

I sigh because, unlike Ven, I won't be getting my rocks off with a beautiful woman.

She collapses to the bed while her body shudders in pleasure. Her moans echo around the room, turning into sobs of rapture. The orgasm was so intense, she's like putty when Ven flips her on her back and straddles her tiny frame. He shoves his cock between her jiggly tits and fucks them, squeezing them together to cocoon his dick. He ruts a few times, then paints her face in white ribbons of cum.

I leave the room, closing the door behind me, but still sense her searching for me long after I've left. "I don't fuck the help, maylshka," I say to no one.

Once in my own room, I rid myself of my armor and shower. The pellets are cold and punishing. Thoughts of Irina assault me at the hardening of my cock. Would she still look at me with such devotion and need if she knew I liked to see a woman's tears before seeing her pleasure?

I doubt it, and she will *never* find out.

Instead of thinking of sweetness and perfection and small nipples through a silky gown, I fist my cock to images of blue lips and giant, jiggly tits. It's not what I want, but it'll do the job.

I force all distraction from my mind and come thinking about control. Whatever it was I'd entertained briefly in my head with Irina was nothing but a small lapse. I am a Vasiliev. We don't lose our control. In fact, we don't lose at all.

It's time to stop thinking like a pussy and start playing like a master.

CHAPTER SEVEN

Irina

Diana is in a heated conversation with Anton when I arrive at her office after a late breakfast. I'm exhausted from last night's revelations. It's not typical for me, but for once, I slept in.

The conversation looks tense if the frustration etched on Anton's features is anything to go by. I slip in and take my seat. Both of them ignore me, but my presence is known. Diana sits behind her large desk and gestures for Anton to leave with a chin tilt.

He doesn't move for a good four seconds. I know because I count them.

Eventually, with an almost imperceptible sigh, he rises and stalks away. His footfalls are heavy with intent to show his displeasure at whatever they've discussed. She probably plans to make him accompany us to the Vasiliev estate. It's not the job he's used to or even suited for, but it's the one he'll do if she orders it. Anton is Father's right-hand man. He does all our father's dirty work and does it with a smile and a nod. So there is no doubt he will comply and accompany us. Diana will make sure Father thinks it's a good idea too. Diana always has a way with men and our father isn't immune to her charm.

"You look tense," I comment, watching her for any

signs of cold feet.

"There's just a lot to prepare for." Her sigh is heavy and resigned. She's no longer the giddy, excited woman from last night.

I stand and walk over to her, sitting on the corner of her desk. "Does Anton not want to play security for us?" I ask in a playful tone, but it doesn't break through her salty mood.

"Anton will do as he's told," she grinds out, her voice cold and unwavering.

Holding up my hands in mock surrender, I make my way back to my chair. "Like we all do," I snip at her.

She slams her pen to the desk. "Not now, Irina. If you're going to be a brat, you can work from your own office."

I gape at her outburst. My eyes drift to the adjoining door separating our offices. I've never used mine. Never. I haven't even been in that office since it was assigned to me by Father over a year ago. She and I work together. It's what we do.

My chest aches, but I call her bluff. I stand and move toward the door. I'll teach Diana that her snapping at me like I'm the help won't be tolerated. Before my hand touches the handle, she rushes over to me.

"Stop," she cries out, her voice cracking. "I didn't mean it." She stands between me and the door, her brows scrunched together in worry.

"I know you didn't," I bite out. "So don't say things you don't mean."

She reaches forward and brushes away my hair, tucking it behind my ear. "Okay. I'm sorry. It's not you." She sighs and touches her lips with her fingertip, her canary-yellow diamond engagement ring reflecting brilliantly. "I'm a little stressed."

I fold my arms and take a couple steps toward my chair. She makes her way back over to her desk. I turn abruptly and open the door to my office. Her gasp is audible, and she rushes over to pull the door closed. Her eyes are so round and bright, they look like full moons.

"I-I-I sleep in there sometimes," she sputters out, her voice wobbling with nerves. "When I'm working late at night."

Although she is quick to close the door, I've already mentally scanned and stored what was inside.

There's a bed expanding from the far wall where my desk was once situated. The covers are in disarray, and if I'm not mistaken—which I never am—there are a pair of panties in two pieces at the foot of the bed.

"Shadow," she says my nickname desperately, and it's then I realize I haven't spoken. When I look up into her penetrating gaze, I see fear. It's not something I've ever seen in Diana's eyes. She's always so sure of herself. So calm and poised. "I just sleep there sometimes when I work late," she repeats, as though saying it again will somehow make me believe those words.

Her room is a few doors away. There's no need to sleep in there. I'm not buying her story.

"Irina, please," she begs, her voice an edgy whisper. I understand the unspoken words in her tone.

Please don't ask questions.

Don't tell anyone.

Never mention this ever again.

Before I can conjure up a thought, screeching echoes down the corridors. I recognize our mother's voice and turn to follow the disruption. My father's deep tone bellows from his office, and when we reach the door, it's ajar. Our mother's sobs bounce through the open space there.

"How could you not have known? He looks just like you," she cries.

"I don't make a habit of looking at servant kids, Olga. Are you telling me you knew?" he growls.

"You think I can't see my own husband's eyes looking up at me? Why do you think I sent them away?"

"Vy kunt!" *You cunt.* His roar echoes off the walls and the crack of his hand connecting with her flesh is loud. I push through the door to see our mother bent over his desk holding her cheek.

Our father's eyes snap to me, then to Diana, who followed me inside.

"What's going on?" I breathe. I scan the scene before me, taking it all in. When my eyes fall on the man standing beside our father, my stomach curdles.

He's so familiar, I recognize him instantly.

Vas.

He was always around us as children. A wretched little brat. His mother was our most valued maid and we loved her. I cried for weeks when Mother told us she'd left to work elsewhere. Now, looking at him, I see our father in every inch of his face, his frame…damn, even his posture is an exact replica.

"Girls, this isn't the way I wanted you to hear this…" Before he can finish, our mother straightens, brushes her hands down the front of her fancy dress, and turns to face us.

"Your father's bastard has returned to the fold, moi do-cheri." *My daughters.* "To take the kingdom from beneath you."

"Enough," Father barks out his warning.

She's always been weak, but in this moment, she is fire and beauty. She is Diana. Fierce and formidable.

"Look at you both," Vas croons, holding his hands out in front of him. "So grown up. So beautiful."

"Otets," Diana breathes. Our father reacts to her pained call and moves toward her, taking her hands.

"I found out recently Vas is, in fact, a result of my indiscretion," Father admits.

"She knows you screw the help," Mother snaps. "They're not blind or stupid." She flinches, all fire snuffed out, when father drops Diana's hands and waltzes toward her.

"Ostorojno, jenshina." *Careful, woman.*

"How long have you known?" I find the words tumbling out of me as the past months play over and over in my head.

"Nearly a year," Vas answers for our father.

Nearly a year? Bastard.

This is why he suddenly wants to pawn us off like chess pieces. He has no need for daughters. He has the son he always wanted. Vomit threatens to spill from my lips. I won't give Vas or our father the pleasure of seeing me fragmenting, my entire childhood scattering and drifting away like smoke from a fire.

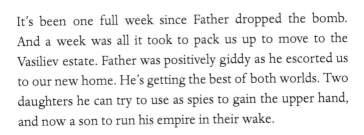

It's been one full week since Father dropped the bomb. And a week was all it took to pack us up to move to the Vasiliev estate. Father was positively giddy as he escorted us to our new home. He's getting the best of both worlds. Two daughters he can try to use as spies to gain the upper hand, and now a son to run his empire in their wake.

I hate him.

I hate Father so much, I could scream.

And all of Mother's fury died once he set her in her place. She retreated to her room and drowned her sorrows in Father's most expensive vodka, chasing pain pills like it was her job. That's good ol' Ma. Hiding behind a haze of numbness while her daughters are sent into the fray to do the dirty work.

As we enter the ornate foyer in the Vasiliev home, I realize this home is anything but the slums. Everything is expensive and well taken care of. Servants peek from around corners, trying to catch a glimpse of the new prizes Vlad has acquired.

That is what we are, after all.

Prizes.

After seeing Vas with my father and the way my mother behaved last week, I find my heart bitter and angry. Diana has retreated into herself, but I'm bubbling with rage. This life Father has created for us is bullshit. Yes, we're spoiled with anything money can buy, but it can't buy happiness. Hell, it can't even buy contentedness. We're moving into the enemy's mansion and we're expected to play nice.

I'm so done playing nice.

"This way," a woman with big boobs and a forced smile says. We follow her through a series of corridors until it opens into a new wing of the house. "This is the north wing. Five bedrooms, five bathrooms, a small kitchenette, a library, an office, and a sitting area. I do hope these accommodations suit you." Another fake smile. "The bathrooms, especially, are quite nice."

Diana nods and smiles back at her. My sister's smile is gorgeous. Fake as well, but gorgeous. "Thank you, darling.

This is more than lovely."

"I'm Rada," the woman says. "Should you need anything at all, please push the button on any of the panels in each room and I will be at your service."

As the woman starts to leave, Diana stops her. "Rada, when will dinner be served? I assume we'll be dining with my fiancé, Mr. Vasiliev?"

Rada's cheeks burn crimson and she purses her lips. "I'm unsure, ma'am. Someone will be around to let you know." Rada bows her head, then scurries off.

"I don't like her," I grumble out.

"You don't like anyone," my sister teases. Despite her forced playfulness, I can sense her apprehension. We're in the lion's den. Vlad may be a gentleman and a longtime friend, but he's still a Vasiliev. Cunning and ruthless. Violent when the situation calls for it.

"I should room between you in case any trouble should arise," Anton grits out. "I'll need to get to you both quickly."

Diana gives him a nod. He stalks off to check out the rooms. I walk over to a leather chair in the sitting room and plop down. My eyes skim over every detail of the room. Dark, thick drapery covers the windows, allowing little to no light in. A fireplace cackles with a fire on one end of the room. Not a speckle of dust jackets anything in the space. The home is clean and immaculate, just not very warm and cozy. It could definitely use some throw blankets and a couple fuzzy pillows.

My sister smirks at me. "Don't," she warns, her lips turning up into a wide grin.

"I'm just thinking," I say with a pout.

"And what color is this thought?"

I let loose a small giggle. "Teal. I mean teal and

chocolate go so well together."

"Oh, dear God," she says, shaking her head. "Can you imagine the look on Vlad's face if he came into this room only to see you've redecorated it to your specifications?"

I stick my tongue at her, earning another laugh. "I just think these big houses are gloomy. All it would take would be a few chenille blankets, a couple faux fur throw pillows, and a splash of color. Voila. Creepy dungeon turned magical reading spot."

She nods and gives me a thankful smile. My sister wants me to try to make this work. For her, I will. I'll never let my guard down, but if she has hopes of finding happiness, I won't stop her. "I'll speak to Vlad," she vows. "Order what you want and I'll convince him to let us spruce up the north wing."

I raise both brows at her. "And what makes you think big, bad Vlad will agree to chenille and teal?"

My sister winks at me. Such a devious wink. "I can be convincing when I want to be."

CHAPTER EIGHT

Vlad

Weapons.

The V Games aren't complete unless we're the proud owners of the best weapons on the planet. Father has sent me after women—dirty little playthings to be used as pawns and distractions for next winter's games—but I'm taking care of my own agenda as well. While he's training used-up whores to be duplicitous sex vixens, I'll be training someone on how to disembowel a man in three seconds flat. The games I play are far more vicious.

I'm training a new someone.

My last someone was ripped right from my grip as of last week.

Anger, furious and explosive, bubbles just below my surface.

In due time, I'll deal with that error.

Vas had always been a deviant shithead, and although I wanted to throttle the little terror when he would torment Irina, I saw the darkness inside him. I wanted to bottle it and take it out when the time was right. He made an excellent trainee when I tracked him down nearly a year ago, already fighting in underground circuits and running his own street crew. He was nothing but a thug, but a cunning one, and willing to learn and train. Perfect.

I taught him everything I knew…

And then Leonid ripped him away now that his blood is actually worth something. Leonid knew he was his the entire time Vas trained with me—they both did—yet they failed to offer that information, instead learning what they could while they could.

In due time, they'll understand their mistake.

"I like this one," I tell Oleg, the arms dealer who's traveled from nearly five hundred miles away to offer me his stash.

"Just one?" he asks, his voice gravelly from too many years of smoking.

"To start," I say as I hold up the knife. It glistens under the overhead light. It's curved like a curled claw with a sharp blade on both sides. The tip is shaped like a fishing hook. Whomever meets the end of this won't live to tell about it. "What else you got?"

My new trainee, Stepan Koslov, from the Second Families, who are deemed lesser than the First Families, doesn't move a muscle beside me. He's every bit as tall and wide as Vas was. Where I thought Vas was just some kid of a housekeeper, I know Stepan's bloodline. His father, Nestor, is a small arms dealer. Nothing of Oleg's caliber, but they are local and good to buy from in a pinch. Stepan runs his mouth a lot less than Vas, which works in his favor. But where Vas moved without hesitation, Stepan is still learning and thinks too long before each move. Stepan may be the older of the two at nineteen, but he's just not quite there yet.

Yet.

I will break him in like I broke Vas.

A ruthless, fighting killing machine.

A winner.

Leonid can go fuck himself when he loses. You can't go nose-to-nose with someone like me and come out unscathed. I *always* win.

I hand the blade to Stepan and he grips the hilt. It fits perfectly in his massive hand. My heart tightens in my chest as I recall handing my brother a blade before he entered The Games just over two months ago. At least with Stepan, I feel nothing for him. He could walk into those Games ten months from now and get gutted like a fish within the first few moments and the only regret I'd have would be that I didn't train someone better.

He *will* be the best, though.

"This one," Stepan growls from beside me as he hands me back the knife. "I like this one."

I give him a nod as I tuck it away inside my jacket and then follow Oleg to another trunk full of weapons. He shows me grenade launchers and guns. Those interest me for selling to the neighbors to the south. Unrelated V Games business. I snap my fingers over the chest and motion for the entire thing.

Oleg lets out an appreciative whistle as we continue "shopping." I pluck unique items that will prove to one day be useful for Stepan along the way. Once I've accumulated enough trunks to satisfy the Kazakhstani mob, I motion for Oleg to follow me. Stepan stays behind, guarding our haul without having to be told. He'll make for a formidable player in The Games. Unlike Vas and Viktor, he obeys my goddamn commands.

I walk out of the garage and into our house. Oleg knows the drill. He brings weapons all the time. My father and him go back to before I was born. Now that I'm more or less in charge, I deal with Oleg. Who the hell knows what Father actually does these days besides meddle in my business. Oleg steals an apple from a basket and I have to listen to his crunching and slurping the entire way to my office. If I were a lesser man, I'd shove the half-eaten fruit down his windpipe and let him suffocate. There's nothing worse than a loud eater. Loyalties or not, one day that bullshit will get him killed.

Once inside my office, Oleg settles his beefy frame in one of the chairs. I walk over to a giant portrait of my father, Vika, and myself. The one that used to include my brother as well has been removed from the premises. I allowed it as a sign of respect for my father, but the rest of my pictures in my office of my brother and I remain. I grab hold of the bottom left of the giant frame and pull it from the wall. Behind the obnoxious painting is my massive safe. While Oleg makes love to his apple, I key in my code and open the safe. Inside is a duffle bag full of money—money that's already been negotiated with Oleg. He knows the drill. I may like to pretend I'm deciding on the weapons, but I end up buying them all.

No man can ever have too much of an arsenal.

I crave to look at the stack of photos at the back of the safe, but now's not the time. Pictures of my siblings and I when we were children are held dear beside my mother's jewelry and Viktor's old wallet. No pictures of my mother exist. All I have left of her is what's in this safe and sketchy memories of her smile. But with my brother's wallet, I can sometimes hold the leather to my nose and inhale the cologne lingering on to it. The memories of him are bolder and still etched into my mind. Fuck, how I miss my brother.

I realize I've stopped to touch the wallet. I stifle a groan and quickly shut the safe. When I turn to regard Oleg, juices run down his stubbly jaw and drip on his shirt. It makes me twitchy to grip his thick throat and drag him from my pristine office. Instead, I take a page from Father's book and ignore what disgusts me. I set the bag of money at his feet and then unbutton my suit jacket. With a quick tug, I pull it from my body and hang it from a hook in the corner.

I'm on edge after seeing Viktor's wallet.

It's a constant reminder that he's gone.

Fury at my sister sets my soul on fire. I wish to tug at my tie and loosen it, but I refuse to show weakness, even in front of a man who wouldn't notice if weakness slapped him in the face. I place my hands on my hips and stand behind my desk, my legs slightly parted. The vest I'm wearing fits snugly over my crisp white dress shirt. I'm uncomfortable and realize I must be spending too much time in the gym training with Stepan. I'm outgrowing my damn clothes.

"The women?" I ask.

Oleg sticks one of his dirty fingers in his mouth and slurps off the juicy remnants. With his eyes on his hand, I allow myself one moment to show my disgust. I snarl my lip up and shake my head. Fucking disgusting. How Father put up with this for decades is beyond me.

"Well," he says, once he's satisfied he's clean. "I've got fifteen out in the truck. Dirty as all fucking hell, but Yuri likes 'em that way. The dirtier the better. Some of dem bitches are even into humiliation." He grabs at his crotch and grins salaciously at me.

"We don't need them *into* anything," I bark. "We need them strong and pliable."

"The money?"

"You know it's already in the bag."

He grunts and raises his hand like he's going to throw his core across the room and into my trashcan. Over my goddamn body.

Before I can open my mouth to threaten him, I lock eyes with a pair of icy blues watching me from a dark corner of my office.

Little Irina.

I'm so stunned by her sudden appearance, I allow the dipshit to throw—and miss, for that matter—his core at my trashcan. He grunts and stands to go pick it up. I can't look away from the little girl hiding in my office, watching my business like it's her God-given right.

She sits primly, wearing a plain, fitted black dress. Her silky blonde hair has been straightened and hangs in front of the swell of her breasts. A black headband keeps the hair from her eyes. To an outsider, they'd think of her as an ordinary girl, barely a woman.

But ordinary girls don't spy on Russian mobsters without fear in their eyes.

No, a challenge dances in her blue-eyed stare. A challenge that, for a moment, speaks right to my cock. It twitches, and I force my stare from her supple, swollen lips. Lips I'd nibble the fuck out of. I'd take that silky hair of hers and wrap it tightly around her slender throat. Watch her eyes gloss over with tears. I'd bring her to the brink of death, only to reawaken her and show her how alive she really is.

"Need to check out the merchandise?" Oleg asks, dragging me from beautiful visions I'd much rather dwell on. His gaze flits over to the corner and he whistles. "Well, I'll be goddamned, boy. Is this the one you're marrying?" He waves, far too friendly for an arms dealer, motioning her to him. "Come here, pretty little thing. Introduce yourself to Uncle Oleg."

I grit my teeth and glower at Irina. I knew the Volkov ladies would arrive today, but I certainly didn't expect to see either of them until dinner. Having her here will prove to be more difficult than I originally thought. Perhaps seeing the skanks out in the truck will help the state of my cock. It would also do well to put my little shadow in her place. Now that they are here, they don't run things as they once did.

They are merely pawns.

Gorgeous pawns, no doubt, but still pawns.

"Come," I bark out and snap my fingers, pointing to the carpet in front of me.

Irina's cheeks flush, but she obeys. That really gets my dick hard. Images of her on her knees in front of me flash. Her blonde tresses tangled in my fist as I skull-fuck her pretty mouth. Slowly, as though her walk itself is meant to seduce me, she makes her way over to me. I notice every detail as she moves. The way she bites her fat bottom lip that I'd love to suck. The way her neck turns slightly pink in my presence. The way her small tits bounce with each step she takes beneath her dress.

Sweet, Irina, you've showed your cards far too soon.

You want me, but you can't have me, my love.

She stops in front of me and looks up. Her nostrils flare as she inhales my scent. It does something to my insides. Basic and male. I have the urge to grip her slender, unmarked throat and squeeze until it bears my memory for days.

Would her plump, pink lips turn blue?

Would she gasp for breath? Claw at my vest and pop the buttons?

Or would she moan and squirm and spread her legs for me?

Would sweet Irina come, my name rasping from her lips that would no longer taste the air?

My cock is impossibly hard, and I don't realize I'm struck simply staring at her until Oleg lets out a chuckle. He may be close to my father, and therefore an ally of mine, but what he just saw is grounds for termination. The permanent kind. I snap my gaze his way, and he raises his hands in surrender.

"I didn't see nothin', kid," he says. "Meet you at the truck." He hurries from my office and out of my sight. Wise man.

"What are you doing here?" I demand, my voice low and deadly. My eyes are still on the doorway because I can't look at her. She weakens me with her stares. So sweet and curious. I can't deal with this right now.

"I came to talk to you. I wanted to ask you something."

"Oh?" I turn and regard her young face.

It wasn't but a few months ago that she was nothing but a child. An untouchable, out of reach child. Still, I fantasized things no man ever should. Dreams of holding her down, spreading her creamy thighs, and shoving inside her tight, virgin heat. Sometimes I wish my world weren't so complicated. I'd give up so much just to have one taste of what others take for granted. Something as simple as fucking a woman you're addicted to, and I am addicted. She holds a power over me, and the pull is getting unbearable.

Her gaze travels to my mouth, then my Adam's apple. She keeps skimming down until her eyes fixate on my vest pocket. Her hand lifts and her slender fingers brush against my pocket as she plucks away a stray fiber. When she goes to drop the fiber, I grip her dainty wrist. It's naked. If she were mine, I'd decorate her delicate wrists with glistening gems.

"Don't put that on my floor," I murmur, my voice husky.

A smile tugs at the corners of her lips. "You'll let *Uncle Oleg* throw half-eaten apples in your office and drip juice all over your chair, but I can't drop a loose thread?"

I would love nothing more than to continue this banter and flirt with the gorgeous girl. Unfortunately, I have a duty and it calls, goddammit. She is the sister of my fiancée. I can't go there. Even if I selfishly wanted to fuck her and take that ripe cherry I know she has all for myself, I can't. Father would have my head if I mess up this marriage arrangement.

"It's high time the Volkovs see how the Vasilievs do business," I bite out, my voice turning cold. I can't bring myself to release her hand. "Tell me what it is you want, then I will make you pay for it by doing something for me."

Her brows furl together as she realizes our moment has dissipated. I wish I could put the smile back on her face, but now is not the time. Possibly never. She tries to tug her wrist from my grip, but I tighten it. If I can't adorn her wrist with jewels, she can wear my bruises instead.

"I need a studio."

I blink at her. "There is an office and I was told Diana and you shared one before—"

"Not an office, a studio." Her cheeks turn a rosy pink as she drops her gaze from mine. "Like the sunroom back home."

To paint.

All fierce determination to stay focused falls to my feet and shatters into a million pieces as my mind whirs with possible studio spaces in my home. I want to keep her far from the south wing where Father resides. Perhaps the west wing instead. I know just the place.

"I'll find you a place," I vow, my voice husky once more.

Her blue eyes lift and glitter with excitement. My heart rattles in its cage. This woman—sweet little Irina—is so bad for me. She distracts me when I need to stay sharp and focused. "Thank you, Vlad."

I stare at her for a beat longer, imagining just how beautiful she'll look with the morning sun blanketing her as she paints in the greenhouse just off the sitting room beside my bedroom. I could watch her without her knowing. Like old times. My cock jolts against my thigh, eager for this notion.

"That's settled," I grit out, driving away all thoughts of Irina painting in *my* house. "Come with me."

Oleg opens the back of the truck and many eyes peer from the darkness. Used, tired, worn out looking women stare back at us. Many are beautiful despite their dirty appearance. Father will be pleased.

I motion for them to follow me. They whisper quietly amongst themselves as they file out of the truck. Irina keeps shooting me death glares, which only serves to harden my resolve. She will do this because it is asked of her. If she expects protection on my part, and a damn studio, then she can do this for me. It makes more sense for a woman to handle it anyway. At least I don't have to worry about any of them ending up pregnant, raped, or mysteriously dead.

Irina huffs, mumbling furious Russian curse words

under her breath.

Okay, so maybe dead…only time will tell.

I walk them around the house to the back where a small shed sits. Inside is a stairwell that leads under the house. Beneath our home is where we train our fighters and whores. The ones who are worthless of manipulation will be sold to the likes of Ven Vetrov and his family. They're always good to traffic a handful of worthless women.

I pull a set of keys from my pocket. The engine of the truck echoes off the snow-covered landscape as Oleg leaves. Stepan brings up the rear, making sure none of the women flee. I'm not sure whether Oleg took these women or lured them here under the guise of better working conditions, but either way, I've paid for them and they're mine.

"I can't believe you bought these women," Irina mutters.

Ignoring her, I unlock the shed and push through the door. I step aside and usher Irina in. Her shoulder, now covered in a thick winter coat, brushes against my chest. If there weren't sixteen people behind us, I'd push her against the dark, dingy shed wall and show her what other nefarious deeds I'm capable of.

I grip her elbow and guide her down the dimly lit stairwell. "This way."

She tries to jerk her arm from mine, but I tighten it. Little Irina is going to wear many of my bruises. We make it to the bottom that opens up into a giant area covered with mats. The walls are lined with rooms used for various things. In the women's case, they will sleep and train here. By train, they will learn to fuck like their lives depend on it.

Because they will.

As soon as Stepan, Irina, and I leave, we'll lock the fifteen women inside. They'll be fed and cared for. They just won't be allowed to leave.

I turn and stare down each one, quickly assessing them. I weed out the good from the bad in one quick glance. And the one cowering behind a thick-waisted woman in the back... well, she's going to be Father's favorite. He likes the small, dark-haired ones. The ones who most resemble girls. The ones who are unable to put up much fight. With a barely stifled sigh, I point at her.

"Name?"

She peers up at me as though I could possibly be her savior. Big brown eyes. Messy hair hiding her from the world around her. "Darya."

"Take Darya to stable one," I tell Stepan. "The rest of you may choose your own stable."

Irina is stiff beside me, but wisely doesn't say a word. When I'm commanding in my element, people bend to my will. They bow at my feet and obey my commands. Even the sweet girl I'd love to spend each day fucking the fire out of.

"Stables? What are we? Livestock?" a mouthy blonde with a ratty fur coat challenges me.

"Call yourselves whatever you want," I sneer. "But you belong to me now. If you're wise, you will train, and you will succeed. If you behave, you'll be rewarded. Simple."

"Doesn't sound very simple at all, asshole," she yells back.

Belligerent bitch.

"Come here," I seethe, my voice low and dangerous.

The woman eyes a chair nearby. With venom in her glare, she picks it up and heaves it toward Irina.

Rage.

Hot, quick, violent.

I don't think as I knock the chair out of the way before

it takes out Irina.

Yanking my new favorite hooked knife from my inside pocket, I lunge for the woman. Slash. Yank. Splatter. So fast. So efficient. I stare down in awe at the bloody, gory mess pouring from her stomach. Her intestines slide from the slices I inflicted and fall to the floor with a slurp. Several women gasp and whimper, but it's a soft sob I recognize that pulls me from my furious haze.

I push the still standing, but quickly emptying example of a woman, and she crumples to the floor. Fourteen women now. Father won't be pleased. However, the high-pitched screams as Stepan locks the young woman into stable one tells me I'll soon be forgiven.

Father loves a screamer.

With blood dripping from my knife, I turn and point it at each woman. They all cower and scamper off to the stables leaving Irina gaping at me in horror.

Sweet Irina, this game is deadly and I always win.

Your stupid father threw you to the wolves.

"Y-You're a m-monster," she rattles out, her teeth clacking together.

I stalk over to her and smear a bloody thumb along her creamy cheek. "As if you did not know this, little Irina."

"She was just a woman—"

I cut her off by pressing my bloody thumb to her plump lips. "I'll only say this once, so listen clearly. I. Do. What. I. Want. She was a whore, bought and paid for, and now she's an example to the other women."

Her blue eyes widen, and she blinks rapidly at me. She starts to pull away from me and the monster she claims lives within me strikes. I snag her dainty throat and yank her to me.

Diana.

The Games.

Father.

I try to focus on all of that, but I can't. All I see is *her*. Irina's pink lips smeared with the whore's blood. Lips that part so she can gasp for air. I lean forward, slightly releasing my grip, so she can suck me in. She needs to learn that I'm her master now. The moment I slid that stone on her older sister's finger and Diana begged me to look after Irina too, *they* became mine. Irina is mine in some capacity, and I can feel my grip on her life tightening like a vise. It makes my cock painfully hard knowing she not only won't be marrying someone of her father's wishes, but she won't be marrying anyone at all. Little Irina will die a pure, delicate virgin because I command it.

If I can't have her perfect cunt, no one else can.

"Sir," Stepan calls out, his voice sharp. It cuts through my haze and I snap my attention his way. He doesn't hide behind cool aloofness like Vas or Viktor. Stepan wears his emotions on his goddamn sleeve. Another lesson I'll have to teach him.

"Yes?" I challenge. He's uncomfortable with me choking the sister of my fiancée. I can see it in his eyes. But he, of all people, knows every level of the game.

"The woman is secure."

"Good. Make sure Father knows where she's being kept," I instruct.

His glare is hard, as if he's imploring me to let Irina go. I'll let her go when I fucking feel like it.

"You're dismissed," I say coldly.

He stays for a beat longer before storming from the basement. I'll chain his ass up later and do like Father used to when the hunting hounds would misbehave. Beat them with a switch until they cried and remained forever submissive.

Some of the rage has bled from my mind and it's then I realize both of Irina's hands grip my wrist of the hand that's around her throat. I'm squeezing only hard enough to keep her in place. Perhaps just hard enough to leave a purple reminder of who the hell's in charge around here.

Instead of finding tears, I catch her staring at me. One of her hands leaves my wrist and she brushes a strand of hair that's fallen from its gel hanging in front of my eye. The heat of her touch speaks straight to my cock. I close my eyes for a moment, relishing in her touch, before I let out a heavy sigh and release her.

"Your duty is to train these women. Diana will be busy doing things I'll ask of her, but this is something you can do. Teach them how to act like a lady. Show them how to dress and behave. Make them take a goddamn bath." I straighten my coat and let my gaze rake over her trembling frame. The blood smeared on her face makes her look even sexier. Images of puncturing her skin with my knife and smearing her blood all over her perfect, young tits has me nearly coming in my slacks.

"If I don't," she challenges, her voice raspy and hoarse.

I raise a brow at her. "Be a good girl. Your studio awaits you."

She purses her lips, but doesn't argue. And when I toss the keys at her, she catches them and pushes them into her pocket.

"I expect you'll be presentable by dinner?" I question, no inflection in my voice. "We'll have many guests attending tonight."

Her gaze flits over to the corpse behind me and she

swallows. "Yes."

"Don't wear anything risqué. I know your sister worries about your virtue."

A flaming in her blue eyes is the only reaction she rewards me.

With a tip of my head, I leave sweet little Irina in charge of fourteen whores and a corpse.

CHAPTER NINE

Irina

I stare at my reflection in the mirror above the dresser in my new room. Everything about this place feels cold. I'm simply an outsider visiting.

More like a prisoner.

My lips are painted with the reddest lipstick I own because I swear, no matter how much I scrubbed my mouth, the woman's blood remained on my lips. A shudder ripples through me. I've seen glimpses of Vlad's power, but never have I seen *that*. What I saw earlier was violent and terrifying. I've seen people kill before—hell, Diana killed a man for hurting me—but it's never been that brutal.

He. Killed. Her.

In cold blood.

Emotionless.

Tears threaten, but I blink them back quickly. I didn't tell Diana about earlier in the basement. Her bedroom door was closed and the music was loud. I was glad Anton's door was closed as well. Neither of them saw me rush past, sobbing my heart out, a disheveled, bloody mess. As soon as Vlad left, I locked up that basement and fled. Guilt sluiced through me at leaving those women, but I'm no idiot. In our world, false moves get you killed in an instant. It doesn't matter who your sister or father are.

People die. "Accidents" happen.

I frown when I notice a purple bruise forming on my throat. I'd chosen a demure black dress where the neckline doesn't go below my collarbone. He'd been clear in his warning. Don't wear anything risqué. Five minutes ago, I heeded that warning because fear threatened to swallow me whole.

But now?

Bravely, I lift my chin and unzip the side of my evening gown. It falls to the floor in a heap, leaving me in nothing but my black strapless bra, lacy thong, and thigh highs. The back of my bra is held together by two thin silver chains, making it perfect for open-back dresses. It shouldn't be hidden behind something so plain. I walk over to the closet and rummage around until I find a dress Diana bought for herself, but it didn't quite fit her larger breasts. It was a little flashy for my tastes, so I never wore it.

I pull the slinky silvery-gray material from the hanger and slide it up my thighs. It's long and fitted, hitting a mere hair above the floor, but has a slit up the side that cuts through the material all the way to my hip. I zip up the side and make my way over to the full-length mirror. The dress dips dangerously low, revealing my quivering breasts that only look this supple and ripe because of the killer bra. The material hangs slightly off my shoulders and sinks low on my back, showing off skin to just above the crack of my ass.

Wow.

I look…

Like a shadow come to life.

The light catches the tiny, sewn-on sequins and sparkles.

I'm a shadow standing in the sun.

My long blonde hair has been pulled up into a fancy

bun, but I decide I want the silky locks down at the last minute. I tug at the pins and free my waves.

I'm beautiful.

The thought makes my heart catch.

Vlad can be a monster, Diana's monster, but for the first time in my life, I feel beautiful and free—free to marry whomever I want.

Maybe while Vlad makes out with my sister—his fiancée—I'll start setting my sights elsewhere. Stepan, a good-looking man I'd been introduced to earlier, wouldn't be a bad one to kiss. I saw the way his eyes followed me around the room.

Diana calls for me from down the hall. I grab some black silky gloves and slide them up my arms. Then, I head out of my room toward my sister. With her back to me as she talks to a nicely dressed Anton, I admire my beautiful sister. She's an angel—a vision—in her fitted white dress that's apt for a princess. Sparkly and innocent. Any man in the vicinity will be thinking dirty thoughts. You can't look at a woman like Diana in a dress like that and not be affected. Anton glowers at her and shakes his head before glancing up at me. When he sees me, his mouth pops open.

"Ready?" I ask as I approach.

"Miss Irina," Anton utters. "Perhaps you'd like to grab a shawl?"

Diana turns and gapes at me. "Oh my God! You look gorgeous! Is that the dress I gave you?" She lets out a squeal of excitement as she rushes around me to inspect all angles.

"Is this okay?"

"No," Anton barks at the same time Diana says, "Yes."

She turns and glares at him. "She's beautiful, and she's wearing the dress."

His jaw clenches, but he doesn't argue. It makes my chest squeeze to see such a fatherly look of worry on Anton's face. He's nearly as old as Father, but he's much more fatherly than our dad could ever hope to be. I mean, he's spent our entire lives looking after us for Father. Anton is a good man and I trust him implicitly. I know Diana does too.

"Will any of the other families be here tonight?" I ask, my voice shaking slightly.

Diana nods. "The Vetrovs will be here. Veniamin, Ruslan, and Vlad's sister, Vika."

We both share a look that has us giggling. Neither of us like Vika at all. Especially Diana. She won't tell me what went on with them when they were younger, but whatever happened, Vika bears anger for my sister.

Diana links her arm in mine and Anton follows behind as we make our way through the corridors to the main hall. As we reach the stairwell, I feel eyes on us. Many eyes. The room below is bustling with guests and waitstaff. As we descend the stairs, they seem to be collectively holding their breath. I search the crowd for Stepan, hoping to catch his eye and find him right off the bat. Diana will go to Vlad, and I'll be left alone. I'm already planning my escape route.

My flesh heats, and I know Vlad's eyes have found us. I try not to look at him, but my eyes betray me. He stands at the bottom of the stairs wearing a mask of indifference. But I see the fire blazing in his amber stare. The same fire that blazed when he disemboweled that woman for talking back. Except, he puts on a show in front of all these people. Even my sister. Our eyes are locked and I nearly stumble. Diana's laughter is like tinkling bells as she clutches onto me to keep me from falling.

Vlad's shoulders are tense and the vein in his neck throbs wildly. Earlier, in his office, I'd admired his physique without his suit jacket on from the shadows. The vest stretched over his impressive chest and the buttons were slightly pulling as though they might go flying off at any moment. And when he turned to enter in the code on his safe, I'd watched in awe at the way his slacks hugged his firm ass that's usually hidden by his jacket. An ass that made my mouth water—that still makes it water.

He ruined it all, though, when he showed me his true colors. I should have known the promise of a studio was nothing but a move in this big game he seems to always play. He gives me what I want, and I give him what he wants in return.

To train them. Such things are beneath my capabilities. Numbers are where I shine. I could be an asset to his empire if he weren't so blind and hardheaded. Perhaps I'll teach his whores math instead. That'll show him.

A shudder quivers through me and Diana stiffens.

His eyes narrow and become more severe as though he can see the thoughts tumbling from my mind. Knowing Vlad, he probably can. He's that good.

"Are you cold? I can send Anton back after your shawl," she says with concern.

"I'm fine," I promise as we reach the bottom.

"Diana. Irina." Vlad's clipped greeting has me diverting my gaze elsewhere. I lock eyes with a handsome man in the corner. God, anything to avoid Vlad's stare right now.

Vlad takes Diana from me and she curls her hand around what I know is his massive bicep. He's changed outfits and not a hair is out of place. You'd never know he slaughtered a woman in cold blood only hours ago. Vlad catches me eyeballing him and smirks. It's brief and only for my eyes. I jerk my stare from him and smile at the cute guy who won't stop looking at me. The guy gives me a head nod and starts in my direction.

"Looks like someone's caught her eye," Diana says to Vlad under her breath, pride in her voice.

Vlad jerks his head toward the guy. "Artur Voskoboynikov," he growls.

"Indeed," Diana agrees, as if an unknown plan of theirs is finally set in motion.

I halt, and Artur strides the rest of the way to me. Tall, lean, muscular. He's handsome, no doubt. Best of all, he seems kind. I could certainly lose myself with a man I'm not afraid will gut me if I step out of line.

"My father didn't lie about the Volkov beauty," Artur says with a wolfish grin.

Vlad sneers. "Perhaps that's the only thing your father never lied about."

Artur takes Vlad's jab as a joke and laughs. Deep, rich, masculine. I find myself warming to him almost immediately. I've heard of Artur—ten years my senior—just never met him in the flesh. His brother, Ivan, who is thirty, though, comes to meetings often with my father.

"Irina Volkov," I say, ignoring the furious heat radiating from Vlad. He wouldn't whip out his scary hook knife and slaughter a Voskoboynikov in front of everyone. Certainly not. "Nice to meet you."

Artur's smile widens and heat prickles through me at having his undivided attention. Is this how Diana always feels? As though everyone's attention is solely on her? He takes my hand and kisses my knuckle over my glove. The heat of his breath through the material sends trembles of excitement stuttering through me.

"Let's eat," Vlad grits out.

Dinner goes on for hours. It's boring and I find myself sucking down wine to pass the time. I'd assumed moving into the lion's den would be more exciting at dinner. Instead, I've listened to family dramas similar to my own and other nonsense for too long. Vlad has finally taken to ignoring me altogether as he flirts with my sister.

They're an item now.

It's what's expected of them.

Diana plays her part well. Blushes at his compliments. Leans in for his gentle kisses to her cheek. Offers her ear when he has a secret only she's privy to. Despite his monstrous slip earlier today, he's back to his usual self. Poised and dapper. Commanding and powerful. Women gaze at him with hearts in their eyes. Men wish they were him.

I'm all but falling out of my chair drunk when I see Artur watching me with a predatory stare. He's hungry for me. Maybe I want to get eaten. A giggle slips past my lips, and Artur smiles back, then motions for me to follow him. I toss my napkin on my plate and stand. The room spins, and I grip the back of my chair to keep from falling. Anton, who sits across from Diana, narrows his eyes at me, but makes no moves to follow. She always was his favorite. Some stand-in dad he is. I roll my eyes at him and try not to stumble out of the busy room where nearly fifty people are dining. I escape into the hallway and see Artur leaning against a pillar.

He lets out a chuckle when I throw myself into his arms.

Strong, capable arms keep me from falling to the floor.

"You are the most exquisite woman I have ever seen," he praises, his hot breath tickling the top of my head.

I look up at him and inhale his masculine scent. It's expensive and manly. Not overpoweringly addictive like Vlad's, but it'll certainly do. Maybe Artur can distract me from my confusing thoughts.

Vlad is a monster. *So why do I still want him?*

I try to kiss Artur's mouth, but bump my teeth against his jaw when I miss. He laughs, the sound husky and adorable.

"Let's find a place to hang out quietly. Show me to your bedroom," he instructs.

I point toward the stairs. When he realizes I can barely walk, he scoops me up. I cling to him as he carries me swiftly up the steps and down the hallway as though he doesn't want anyone to see. Anyone like Vlad. Terrifying images flit through my drunken haze as I envision what sort of things someone like Vlad would do if he knew what was about to happen under his roof. Would he be angry with me? Would this be the nail in the coffin for him to extinguish any apparent attraction toward me and focus solely on my sister? I decide that's what needs to happen. I'll make out with Artur, maybe see where the night takes us, and move on from Vlad.

"There," I murmur, my voice a thick slur.

He carries me inside my bedroom and starts to close the door, but I stop him. A quiver of fear darts through me.

"Leave it open."

His gaze darkens. "Kinky. I like it."

I'm tossed onto the bed and the room spins. My dress has slipped down, and my bra is showing. He peels off his jacket, then tugs at his tie. Things are moving too fast, and

I don't feel so well. I close my eyes to keep from vomiting. Someone clears their throat, violent words are whispered, and then the door closes.

"Hey," I groan, squinting up. "Keep it open."

"Were you hoping I'd see Artur Voskoboynikov, of all people, fucking my fiancée's little sister?" Vlad growls, malice in his tone. "I don't think so."

I stare in horror as he pulls out the same curved knife from earlier. Shiny and pristine. No longer dripping in that woman's blood. He takes a step toward the bed and I sit up on my elbows, quickly assessing my escape routes. His eyes follow mine to the bathroom and he shakes his head.

"There is no escape, little girl. You've messed up and you need to be punished," he hisses.

"I can see whoever I want," I bite back, anger surging through me.

He strikes out with his hand and grabs my ankle, yanking me toward him on the bed. I scream and kick, but the moment the hooked end of the knife presses against my thigh where the slit of my dress ends, I freeze.

"Little Irina," he says, his voice dripping with fury, "you see no one. Absolutely no one. You will die a little lonely virgin who lives in my house."

The fabric rips as he begins slicing upwards. The blade nicks my hip, and then he turns it toward my stomach. I'll die on this bed. He'll cut me open like that woman and I'll bleed out right here. My poor sister.

"Do you understand the rules?" he snarls, making sure the blade scrapes in a threatening way along my flesh beneath the dress as he cuts through it.

"Y-Yes," I breathe, a sob catching in my throat.

He continues shredding the beautiful dress until he

makes it to the neckline. He slices through it, and the silky parts fall to my sides, baring my undergarments to him. His gaze is lazy as he rakes it along my breasts, stomach, and between my thighs.

"You're more than welcome to pleasure yourself as you think of me," he murmurs, teasing my nipple through the fabric of my lacy bra with the tip of the knife.

"I hate you," I choke out.

He arches a brow and shrugs. "But you *belong* to me."

"I belong to no one. Diana said you agreed on that—"

Before I can utter another word, he pounces on me, his heavy body smashing mine against the bed. His strong hand is on my throat again and his nose is inches from mine. God, his smell is intoxicating. I hate myself for being drawn to him even when he's being a lunatic.

"She belongs to me, therefore *you* belong to me. Simple."

I struggle against him, but he manages to wedge himself between my thighs. His hard body pressed against mine brings up so many dirty fantasies over the years, I'm having trouble focusing on why I'm angry because all I notice is the way my core throbs with need.

With a gentle thrust, he grinds his erection against my center. I'm dizzy and drunk and seeing stars of bliss. No longer afraid of him and driven by blind lust, I try to lift my hips, seeking more friction. Slowly, as though he's punishing me, he rocks against me, rubbing in just the right spot. Pleasure is building, and I'm desperate for it.

"Vlad," I whimper.

His fierce amber eyes pin me in place. For a moment, his mask has slipped and the wildness that dances inside comes raging to the front.

Bucking. Bucking. Bucking.

He bucks me right off the cliff of my mind.

I cry out in ecstasy as a quick orgasm steals over me. My entire body trembles from the force of it. Vlad's glare softens as he glances at my lips. Then, cold and uncaring, he's back to being himself as he abruptly pulls away.

"Wear a dress like that again and I'll cut it off in front of our guests. Don't test me, little Irina." He stalks toward the doorway, but stops with his back to me. "Touch Artur Voskoboynikov again and I'll gut him at your feet." He turns to give me a sinister smile. "You." He points with his vicious knife. "You belong to me. Even if I never use you. You are mine."

Without another word, he slips away.

I toss my ruined dress to the floor and curl into a fetal position, cursing the world I've been delivered to.

CHAPTER TEN

Vlad

Artur is lingering in the foyer when I come down the stairs. He paces the floor and stops when he sees me. "I wasn't going to take advantage of her. I'm not that way and you know it. I like her," he defends. He's met her all of once and suddenly he "likes her."

"You don't know her," I bite out, correcting his mistake.

"Well, I would *like* to get to know her. We could be a good match," he offers, his expression earnest.

I have to school my features. I want to cut his tongue from his head and his touchy-feely hands from his arms, but I cannot let my emotions show. I refuse to let it slip that Irina belongs to me even if I can never have her the way I desire. The way *she* desires. Her face coming undone beneath me just now is scarred into my memory forever. It's something I'll visit to spill my seed to when Diana isn't fulfilling my needs.

"She's not looking for a match or losing her virginity in a drunken haze. You should know better than pulling this stunt under my roof, Voskoboynikov. Out of respect to your brother, I'm going to allow you to leave here with a warning and not a thrashing to teach you some respect and manners."

He swallows, his Adam's apple bobbing. There's irritation in his squinted eyes, being my elder and all, but he knows better than to challenge me.

"Oh, there you both are," Diana sings as she comes floating toward us in her angelic white dress. Her dog is not far behind, lingering in the background. I used to have respect for Anton. He's been with Leonid a long time and is a ruthless killer, but this new assignment is beneath him and laughable. His displeasure is evident.

"Where is Irina?" she asks, coming to stand by my side.

"She retired to her room," Artur informs her. "I'm just leaving, but can you give this to her for me? Perhaps tomorrow when she wakes?" Artur hands Diana a business card with his details emblazoned on it in overly fancy fonts. He tries too hard. Pathetic.

The smile that lifts Diana's lips could make the sun look dim. "Of course, Artur. I'm sure she'll be delighted to give you a call." She flashes me a look that tells me she's thrilled for her sister.

Good luck waiting for that call to come.

He returns her enthusiasm with a megawatt smile of his own, showing all his bought veneers, before leaning forward and kissing her cheek.

"Vlad," he grunts with a nod in my direction, then takes his leave.

Challenge accepted. Foolish man.

"I should check on Irina." Diana touches her hand to my chest and starts to move past me to the stairs. I curl my hand around her wrist softly and let it slip into her palm, halting her. "I already did. She's sleeping. Leave her be and finish the evening with me."

Her long lashes bat as she reaches up to press her lips to the corner of my mouth.

"I'm actually tired myself," she admits with a yawn. "I'd

like to retire to my room if that's okay."

"Of course." I smile tightly as she pulls away and disappears up the stairs. I turn to find Anton behind me. He doesn't say anything. He's always known his place in this world. He nods his head in acknowledgement, then traces Diana's steps.

I look down at the card I slipped from Diana's hand and rub my thumb over Artur's number. Then I rip the card into pieces.

When I get back to the dining room, everyone has left. All but Ven, Rus, and Vika. Ven is typing on his cell phone while Vika talks animatedly to him. He's not listening and it's pitiful. Quite laughable, in fact. Rus's eyes bore into her, but she's too self-centered to even notice she's upsetting her husband-to-be. Not that she'll care either way.

"Vika!" I bark.

Annoyance ignites in her amber eyes at my presence. She swivels her head in my direction, then sits back in her chair, folding her arms over her chest like a petulant child. Her tits bulge out the top of her dress for all to see. Images of her as a small child chasing after Viktor replay in my mind, but diminish as quickly as they came.

She's not that girl anymore and Viktor is gone.

"Join me for a night cap," I tell her. It's not a request, it's a damn order, and she knows it. She's not married yet. Her huff is audible, as is the chair scraping across the floor.

Her heels click-clocking across the hardwood floors alert me to her following my order. I walk to my office. It's the only place that, until this afternoon when Irina invaded the space, was private and just for me.

"What do you want, Vlad? I know this isn't pleasantries." She brushes her hand over one of the tall bookshelves adorning the back wall. Her nose turns up as she pretends to wipe dust from her hand. "This place is really going downhill. You should hire some help who knows how to actually clean and not just polish cock."

"Your vulgar mouth is still intact I see," I sneer, taking a seat behind my desk.

She makes a *humph* sound before crossing her arms and waltzing over to my desk, ignoring the chair situated opposite it. She sits on the corner instead, knocking over a pen holder with a clatter. "Did you think sending me over there would somehow tame me, brat?"

My skin feels too tight over my bones. There's a dull ache throbbing at my temples. I'm done with this day. I cast a glance over her attire and answer her question.

"I know it hasn't stopped you from flaunting yourself all over Veniamin like one of Father's prized whores."

Her eyes narrow and her lips twist up at the corners. "Jealous?"

Jealous? What a ludicrous thing to say.

"Of my sister? Doubtful. You know better than that, Vika." I almost chuckle, but that would be a reward for her. She doesn't deserve a reaction of any kind.

There's a devious glint in her eye as she leans over my desk and whispers, "Not of me. Of him. He does appear to get all the girls."

I'm not sure what game she's trying to play, or what she's implying. Veniamin is a good-looking man who has never struggled to find bed partners. This isn't news to me, and I certainly don't care. We've shared many dirty games ourselves. "Is there something you're trying to tell me and failing miserably at, Sister?"

"I'm just saying Ven has an appeal even the prim of us

can't deny. Why don't you ask your *fiancée* what she thinks?" With that, she smirks and gets to her feet before striding out of my office like she owns the place.

What the hell did she mean by that? I refuse to let her rile me up. It's what she intends, and I'm not that easily played. I will ask Diana what she meant by her words and she will tell me. It's Vika being Vika. Ven would have mentioned if Diana had made any passes at him. *Wouldn't he?*

Tapping into the monitors of Diana's bedroom, I see her bed rumpled and the sound of her shower blasting. My finger hovers over the feed for Irina's room and my head swarms with a thousand bees. She evokes such a response in me, I don't even think she's human. How can she have such power over me?

My finger clicks on the feed, and her room expands, filling the screen. She's sprawled over the bed, her dress discarded in strands on the floor, and she's still in her panties, bra, stockings, and high heels. What a vision she is. Her blonde locks fan out around her like a halo, but she's no angel. She's a seducer, a succubus waiting to pounce and suck out all my willpower. Slipping my cock from slacks, I rub the liquid building on the tip with the pad of my thumb. I want to use my teeth on her, mark her skin, cause blemishes to raise and sting. My handprints will look wonderful on her precious, virgin skin. I hope she's a moaner. I'll torment her body, drive her to the brink of euphoria and drag her back screaming and pleading for more. My tongue will taste every inch of her, plundering into her tight little hole and stretching her. Her groans will shatter into wails of ecstasy.

Squeezing my shaft to almost the point of pain, I release it and stuff it back into my slacks. I have a fiancée for this shit. Getting to my feet, I march up the stairs and slip into

Diana's room. The shower is still blasting, but turns off a few seconds later. Her movements sound through the open door, but I don't push it open to catch a glimpse.

She will show me everything in time.

What a good little wife she will be.

I rap my knuckles on the bathroom door and hear her sigh. "I thought you were mad at me..." she stutters the last words when she sees me standing there.

"Why would I be mad?"

She blinks a couple times, then shrugs her petite shoulders. Water pebbles over her tanned flesh. She's darker skinned than Irina. It's not sun exposure, it's natural. Irina is like a porcelain doll, precious and not to be played with.

"Because I'd had enough of entertaining," Diana says, looking warily at the door behind me.

"No one saw me come in here, and we are to be married," I assure her, hoping to soothe her worries as I place my hands on her bare arms and guide her over to the bed. I sit and gently maneuver her between my legs. Taking my hands from her, I study her form, from her toes, toned calves, thicker thighs, and then towel.

Reaching up, I touch the fabric she clutches onto like it's a raft and she's drowning.

"Let go," I order.

She swallows deep, her lips twitching in desperation to defy me. But I stare her right in the eye. Not dropping it now would be to lose.

Diana is a winner like me.

She releases the towel, and it pools at her feet. Her body is exactly what I expected. The clothes she wears each day display the curves beneath them. Not much is hidden from the imagination. Her hips are round, dipping into a small waist and curving up to accommodate her large breasts. They sit heavy and full, the darker nipples peaking with the chill in the air.

"Turn around," I order.

Her defiance shows itself in her tense jaw. With flushed cheeks, she bends down and retrieves her towel. "I'm not a toy or yours to command, Vlad. You know I want to wait for our wedding night." She moves toward the bedroom door and flicks the lock, locking us inside.

"Are you a virgin?" I ask outright.

She rests her head on the door for a few silent beats, then turns. The businesswoman mask is in place. "If I wasn't, would we be here?"

That would depend on how many lovers she's taken to her bed, but a virgin is rare these days in women of her age, no matter how under the thumb and restricted her options were.

Her father believes her to be, and a virgin is appealing to any man. He would be a liar if he said otherwise. To explore a woman who's never been touched is like finding a treasure map. Irina is such a thing, and I want to watch her bloom under my hand. To coax all kinds of sounds from her lips. To watch her open up like a rose on a hot summer's day is a prize that is so often wasted.

"Vlad." Diana summons me back to reality. "Would it matter to you?"

"Tell me about Veniamin," I demand, ignoring her question.

She's taken back by my line of questioning, confusion wrinkling her forehead. "What about him?"

"Have you made advances toward him in the past?"

"Is this an interrogation?" she snaps. "No, Vlad, I've

never made advances toward Veniamin. Is that what he's told you?" She paces the floor in front of me, then stops abruptly, breaking into a surprised laugh. "Oh my God, did he tell you we kissed? Is that what this is all about?"

"You kissed?" I hiss, rising to my feet. "You kissed Veniamin?"

"Years ago, Vlad, when we were younger. It was because of Vika pestering him all the time. We did it so she would leave him alone. It was nothing. And for the record, she didn't leave him alone."

Vika, the little snake, worming her way into my mind and polluting it with her venom again.

"Are you a virgin?" I ask again.

She huffs out an exasperated breath, and snaps. "Yes, Vlad, I'm a virgin. Happy?"

Yes.

"It wouldn't have been a deal breaker," I say, moving past her.

Lies.

It most certainly could have been a deal breaker.

I need someone's utmost loyalties, in and out of the bedroom.

I lean down and peck a chaste kiss to her lips, then I unlatch the lock and open the door. Anton is standing directly outside, staring at me with a look of surprise.

"Sorry, sir," he utters. "I was just coming to check to see if Miss Volkov retired for the evening so I could retire as well."

"She has," I tell him, watching his eyes flit over my shoulder, knowing what he's seeing.

"Right," he grunts.

And with that, I close her door and hunt down Vika.

CHAPTER ELEVEN

Irina

Bright.

It's too bright in here.

There's a marching band inside my head. I balk when my hand skims my bare stomach. Bolting upright, I observe the room and my near nakedness. I frown when I see I have one shoe still on. Rubbing my eyes, I think back to last night, but draw a blank. I remember dinner and then... nothing.

God, I hope I didn't make a fool of myself in front of all those people.

Scooting to the end of the bed, I notice material littering the floor and I pick up a strand. My dress from last night.

Why would I cut it up?

There's a light tap on the bedroom door and I quickly scan the room for my robe. It's slung over the chair where I left it the evening before. The door is closed, and it makes my nerves ricochet inside my skin.

I hate the door being closed.

I have this reoccurring nightmare of a man coming into my room when I was ten, locking my door, and climbing into my bed. His hand, real as the day lighting this room. I can feel the heat, the hairs on his arm, as he snaked its way inside my underwear.

Diana, at sixteen, was also in my dream—she'd fallen asleep in my reading chair after binge reading the *Twilight* saga with me. Her presence startled him, and he retreated from my room, like a creeping shadow. The dream is still so vivid, I'm not sure whether it really happened or was just that—a dream. A very bad dream.

Slipping on my robe, I move to the door and open it. Diana is on the opposite side holding a steaming mug and a wicked grin.

"I thought you may need this," she says as she hands me the cup and moves past me into the room.

"My head hurts," I complain, joining her as she takes a seat on the bed.

Her gaze darts to the mess of fabric on the floor. "What happened?"

Shrugging, I crinkle my nose. "Maybe it got stuck so I tore it?" I surmise and sip down the hot liquid.

"You look like hell." She smiles, reaching out to try to tame my bed hair.

"You look perfect." I roll my eyes.

She always looks perfect, and today is no different.

"I had a visitor in my room last night." She looks down at her lap, then crosses her legs. My heart begins pounding in my chest. Diana is going to tell me she and Vlad made love. Describing it in incredible detail, as if it were me experiencing it all and not her. I'm not sure I can handle knowing the details. It would truly mean there will never be anything between us. It's such a juvenile and silly thing to think. I despise myself for even having the thoughts, but they're not mine to control. They're just inside my head. I'm a slave to the chemicals inside my blood telling me I need him.

"Vlad," I croak out.

She stiffens a little, then relaxes back, laying down and staring up at the tall ceiling.

"Yes, of course, Vlad. Who else would visit my room?" She lets out a defeated breath, frustration in her tone. "He asked if I'm a virgin."

A snort, unattractive and uncontrollable, breaks free from me. "He what? What times are we living in, Diana? What a ridiculous thing to ask."

She sighs and looks over at me. "You know there's nothing normal about our upbringing, Irina, my sweet little shadow. How determined you are to be a free spirit." She smiles, genuine fondness and love reaching her eyes. I put my mug on the bedside table and curl up next to her, twiddling her soft strands of silky hair between my fingers.

"Well, you *are* a virgin, so that should have pleased his ego," I tease.

Her body becomes tense next to me. I look up at her face and see tears building in her eyes.

"Diana?" I whisper.

She turns her body toward me and holds me so tight, my ribs feel like they may crack under the pressure.

She's not a virgin.

"Don't tell anyone," she pleads into my ear.

I hold her back, squeezing just as tight. "I won't. I promise."

"Why is she limping like that?" I ask Stepan, pointing to the girl Vlad separated from the others when they first arrived. Darya, I think was her name. She's walking like she crapped herself and there's bruising on her cheek.

If these women are supposed to be appealing to perverts and predators, then the beatings will be a problem. No man wants to fulfill a fantasy with an already disfigured, used and abused whore. She's supposed to be a seductress and she can't even walk properly.

"That would be because my father took her out to play with," Vika croons over my shoulder. I didn't even hear her approach. She slithers her way around undetected.

"Vika, I didn't realize you still lived here." I smirk at her. It's catty, but I do love seeing her hackles raised.

"Oh, my name is still Vasiliev, little shadow. I can come and go as I please." She points to the woman limping back to her cell. They can call it a room, but that's sugarcoating what it really is. "She can be put with the rest of the cattle, Stepan. My father won't be back for seconds."

"Cattle, Vika?" I shake my head in distaste. "Really?"

Her cackle echoes off the walls and pounds into me mockingly. "Oh God, Vlad must love having you around here. Sweet innocence is such a rare thing these days." She reaches out to me with a slender finger and strokes down the side of my face.

"I heard your happy news," I snip back. Two can play this game. I remove her finger and cross my arms to defend myself from looking so fragile. Snakes eat their prey when they see weakness.

I am anything but weak.

I am a Volkov.

"Ruslan Vetrov," I sneer. "Wow. How old is he again? Like fifteen?"

Her hand snaps out and fists a handful of my hair, tugging my head back and closing the space between us so her body brushes against mine. "My brother likes to play games. He underestimates me. Viktor did too, and look what happened to him. Careful, little girl, you don't want me for an enemy."

Heels clacking across the stone floor draw Vika's attention. My mind races with all the information she just dropped on me. Did she have something to do with Viktor's death? No, she wouldn't. Surely. He was her twin brother. Why?

"What's going on?" Diana asks, coming to my side. Cool, calm, and collected. Together, the Volkov women are a powerful front.

Vika releases my hair, but Diana grabs her wrist before she can fully retract it. She moves between us, getting right in Vika's face.

"I've killed men for less, Vika," Diana snarls, her perfect red lips curled up in hatred. "Don't ever put your hands on my sister again or you'll lose them *both*. You'll have to wear Ruslan's ring on a chain around your neck like the dirty little dog you are." Diana's tone is ice cold. Violent and threatening. My sister means every single word.

Vika snatches her arm back and scoffs before pushing past us, leaving the same way she arrived.

"What the hell was that about?" Diana hisses, turning to me.

I let out a huff and smooth my now tangled hair. "She's just a bitch. We already knew this."

"Don't provoke her, Irina," she warns. "She is cunning."
You have no idea.

She looks at our surroundings and blanches. "Anton said you were down here. Why?"

"Curiosity? Boredom? Pick one." I don't tell her that her

fiancé is bargaining with me. If I want a studio to paint in, I have to earn it.

She frowns, her brows furrowing as she regards me, not buying my bullshit story for a minute. Thankfully, she lets it slide. "Well, I need to go back to Father's. I've been locked out of all the business accounts and I can't reach him on the phone."

That's strange.

"I'll come with you," I say, but she waves me off. "No, no, stay here. I'll take Anton. I know you don't want to see Father right now."

"Are you sure?"

"Yes, just don't stay down here," she murmurs as she casts another disapproving glance around.

"Okay."

She gives me a peck on my cheek before leaving me with Stepan.

"Stepan, get that girl some medical help," I murmur. "She's useless to us like this."

"The doctor is on his way to check all the women, ma'am."

Ma'am?

"Please call me Irina, or Shadow." I smile, and he stares at me like I've spoken Chinese.

"Why Shadow?" he asks, lines crinkling around his narrowed eyes. He's unnerving. There's a darkness there, sitting behind those deep eyes. I think he's handsome, yes, but he doesn't hold a candle to Vlad.

"It's a nickname," I offer with a shrug, feeling my cheeks heat. "Because I'm in the shadow of my sister, Diana." Oh God, it sounds so pathetic speaking the words out loud.

"That's stupidest thing I've ever heard." He snorts. He's

not mocking me—he means it. "You could never be in any-one's shadow. Look at you," he says with conviction. My stomach rolls.

What does that mean?

"Irina," Diana calls from the stairway. "Come on."

I bow my head and turn to follow her.

"I'll be back for dinner, okay?"

It's only lunchtime, which means Diana is planning to be gone all afternoon. I'm already bored.

"Go find out what's going on," I encourage, even though there's a stone in my gut growing rapidly. Our father is pulling back on all that was given to us. We're the reason Volkov Spirits is as booming as it is. That was our project. Our venture. Unfortunately, he still holds the key to every-thing. He wasn't that stupid to turn over all rights to us.

If he takes all our power, what will we have left?

She pulls her jacket on and Anton hands her a scarf. "You're sure you don't mind Anton driving me?"

"I'll be fine, Diana, go." I practically shove her out the door and sigh when it closes behind her.

"Irina." I startle at my name being barked from the bal-cony above me.

My eyes lift to see Vlad standing there holding the rail-ing. "Come here," he instructs. The brat in me wants to taunt him and ask him to say please, but as much as he ex-cites my blood, he has an authority I can't deny. I take the steps up slowly, counting them in my head.

One…two…three…

My heart flutters in my chest, and I take my time dragging my hand along the bannister as I climb.

Four...five...six...seven...eight...

Gradually. Deliberately. Demanding his attention, even if only for a short while.

Nine...ten...eleven...twelve...

I know it will frustrate him, but I just can't seem to help myself.

Thirteen...fourteen...

Vlad.

Our eyes meet when I reach the top. His ablaze with emotion—a complete contradiction to the impassive expression he wears so well.

Pausing, caught in his gaze, I regard him with an innocent smile.

I've got your attention now.

CHAPTER TWELVE

Vlad

I need a guard at this door to stop just anyone from walking in here.

Fucking Vika. Why does she insist on grating my last nerve? Doesn't she have Ruslan for that?

"So, you get two for one, I see," Vika snaps as she waltzes into my office. She narrows those golden, familiar eyes on me, and I try not to suffocate on her cloyingly sweet stench swirling into my office along with her.

It hurts to look at her sometimes. She has so many of Viktor's features.

"Vika, what an unpleasant surprise."

"Your little pet is making herself quite at home," she continues, ignoring my jab.

"If you're referring to my fiancée, I'd tread carefully. She has more rights here now than you."

"Not Diana," she sneers. "The other one. The little shadow."

Irina.

"They come as a packaged deal. What business is it of yours?" I mock, relaxing back in my chair and busying myself with my cell phone.

"Rus told me what I was traded for. Land, Vlad? Seriously, is that all I'm worth to Father?"

Placing my cell down on the desk, I look up at her, searching her eyes for the little girl I once knew. She was extinguished long ago. Instead, this entity stands here with her eyes.

"Less," I taunt. "I bargained for more, not because I believe you're worth more, but because I can. You are just a puppet, and I'm the master holding the strings. Stop fighting the inevitable, Vika."

"And what is that, dear brat?"

"Retribution. For me, for Niko, for Viktor."

"Sdelay eto svoim metodom, brat." *Have it your way, brother.*

She leaves my office like a storm, tearing through it and knocking over decorations as she goes.

I pick my cell phone back up and continue to scan through the pictures sent to me on a secure server. We have our whores who will be trained in seduction, but The Games are all about the chase. The depravities that lie within us all. Young women, innocent and frightened, are one of the mass appeals for The V Games, and that's something you can't train into someone. These women come at a cost and via special selection. Plucked from their lives and forced into a nightmare.

The faces looking back at me through the screen are that of girls living their life. They have no idea they won't be making it home today if I approve it.

Vika's words regarding Irina play in my mind and I find myself leaving my office and taking the stairs to see how her studio is coming along. The designer arrived an hour ago to assess the room and draw up a plan. Diana mentioned she was going to the Volkov estate for the afternoon. Maybe Irina has gone with her.

The room is so close to mine, if both our doors are left open, I can see straight into the studio. I want to see all her colors displayed through her art. It will be something for me—a wedding gift, if you will.

If I can't have her, I'll just admire from afar.

And no one will have her.

"Mr. Vasiliev, I was just finishing up and coming to find you." The tall blonde woman, Marina, was the one who designed most of the rooms within this house. She was my first call after Irina's request.

"I've saved you the trouble." I offer her a tight smile and take the plans she's drawn up from her hand.

"It's a perfect space, and the light really works well for the intended use."

"I'll look this over and let you know of any changes. I want this started today," I inform her.

Marina's eyes widen, but she nods enthusiastically. "Of course. I'll make some calls."

As I reach the top of the stairs to head down to my office, voices sound from below, stopping me as I listen. Diana hasn't left yet.

"I'll be back for dinner, okay?"

"Go find out what's going on."

Pause.

"You're sure you don't mind Anton driving me?"

"I'll be fine, Diana, go."

The door closes, and I look down to see my little sun blowing a strand of hair from her face.

"Irina," I bark.

Her frame jolts and her icy blue eyes lift, colliding with mine.

"Come here," I demand.

She purses her lips like she's fighting to keep words from spilling free, then moves to obey. Good girl. She takes her time climbing the stairs, dragging her hand along the railing as she almost sways toward me.

"Vlad," she greets. Her voice is warm, and I want to tell her to stop…just stop being her.

"Your bedroom has been moved."

It's spontaneous and out of my mouth before the thought has even manifested fully in my mind. Just looking at her and thinking of last night, I need her closer. To make sure no one else thinks they can creep up to her room with her.

"Wh-What?" she stutters. "But Anton—"

I hold my hand up to cut her off. "Anton was too busy being your sister's lapdog to even notice you'd disappeared to your room with Artur Voskoboynikov. If I hadn't intervened when I did, you would have been birthing his child nine months from now." There's rage in my tone. The friction of my emotions is starting to chafe causing a crack in my demeanor.

Her mouth drops open, forming a small O. The rush of red blossoming over the pale of her cheeks reminds me of when she came undone from my simple contact last night.

So precious. So pure. So mine.

"Thank you," she breathes, taking me aback.

Thank you?

"I shouldn't have drank so much wine. It doesn't agree with me. I'm so terribly embarrassed at my behavior. I don't even remember that happening."

She wraps an arm across her waist and twists at her earlobe with the other hand—a nervous habit I've come to adore.

"Come to my office." I change the subject. She doesn't remember last night. Doesn't remember me cutting away her dress and bringing her over the edge of bliss with just a press of my crotch to hers. Probably better that way.

"You called me up here to tell me to come downstairs?"

The coy little girl has left, and the spunky Irina is back in her rightful shoes.

I want to force her to hold the railings with both hands and bend over so I can smack her tight ass until it burns crimson under my palm. Then I'd use my tie around her neck as a harness while I entered her raw and hard. She'd want to scream out in pleasure, but my hands tightening the fabric would restrict her. People would come and go through the front door, unbeknownst to them that the sweet little virgin sister of my bride-to-be was being schooled on who owns her.

I'll take, take, take from her until her legs give out.

Take her purity, her ripe, cerise cherry, her voice, her orgasms, her heart, her fucking soul. All for my own.

"Vlad?" She bites her bottom lip, and I snap out of the fantasy, sending me into a lust-filled haze. "Why do you look at me like that?" Her voice is a curious whisper, speaking straight to my cock.

"Like what?" I rasp.

Her chest lifts with a deep intake of air. "Like you're hungry and I'm a cake."

A genuine smile lifts the corners of my mouth. Real. What a perfect analogy. I bet she will taste sweet too, like cherry frosting.

"Because you look at me like you *want* to be tasted," I reply, bringing the pad of my thumb to her lips and stroking across them. All the black, damaged evil inside me dilutes when I'm touching her—the sun casting out the darkness inside me.

I expect her to pull away, as she should, but she doesn't. Instead, she wraps her hands around mine and opens her mouth, sliding my thumb inside. Her mouth hot, soft, and wet, sucks as her eyes close and she sighs.

"Mr. Vasiliev, good, you're still here," Marina calls from behind me.

Irina's eyes spring open and she removes me from her mouth. Dropping her hands, she turns to jog down the stairs.

"What?" I bark, turning my glare on the woman.

Marina's feet falter and she turns white. "I'm sorry. I just wanted to inform you that I have movers coming in to clear the space ready for decorating tomorrow."

"Good." That's all she gets for interrupting the delicious moment with my little addiction. I stalk away from her toward my office. Once I step inside, I call Danill, my acquirer of the female cargo specially selected.

"Da." *Yes.*

"Ya vozmu ix vsex." *I'll take them all.* I end the call without waiting for a reply. Who I don't put in The Games, I'll sell to someone else. I already have buyers in mind.

"More women?" Irina inquires from the corner of the room, startling me.

If my father knew she was involved with any business in the Vasiliev empire, he would order me to put her in her place. On her knees. And anyone else, I'd agree with him.

But she's not just anyone.

She's holding a picture, tracing the image with her finger. She doesn't press me when I ignore her question. "No one speaks about him," she says, getting to her feet and walking over to one of the bookshelves. She places the frame down, and it's then I notice which one. A picture of Viktor and I a year ago, at his graduation. The pit opens in my stomach and I will it to close.

Goddammit, I miss him.

"It's still raw for some of us." My words are cold despite the gaping wound in my chest.

"Vika lost two people that day," she muses, looking at other pictures displayed around the office.

"*We* lost two people that day."

She looks over at me. "I'm sorry. I forgot how close you and Niko were."

I don't want to talk about this. I can't. "Here," I tell her, holding out the designs for her studio.

She takes cautious steps toward my outstretched hand and lifts the paper from me. Her sparkling blue eyes skim it, and then lift to mine, a smile spreading across her pretty face.

"A studio?" she asks in astonishment.

If I'd known it would illicit such a breathtaking smile, I would have had a thousand studios made for her.

"Vlad," she cries out, a joyful squeal erupting from her as she jumps toward me. I have no choice but to catch her. Her small frame molds to mine like she was created to fit there. Her hair tickles my cheek and jawline, and the scent explodes into my senses.

Honeysuckle.

Sliding down my body and standing on her feet, she looks up at me though her lashes. "Thank you."

Her lips draw me in, and I can't think straight. All I see, hear, smell, is her.

Dammit.

"I'm going to kiss you," I tell her, my voice matter of fact.

I'm going to ruin everything.

I'm going to ruin her.

Her eyes widen. "You're marrying Diana."

"I know," I grit out, frustration in my tone. "But just this once. Just one kiss." I say it more to me than her.

She bites on her plump bottom lip and I'm desperate to bite it too. This *ordinary* girl does extraordinary things to me.

"I can't Vlad," she breathes, a small pout in her tone. "She's my sister. It's so wrong." Clearly, she misunderstood me. I wasn't asking her.

"Then say no." I challenge her with a glare. For a moment, I think she'll relent. Her lips part, but then she blinks away her daze.

"No." She lowers her eyes. I grasp the back of her neck and tug her body into mine, loving the way her pert tits press against my firm chest. Clutching her jaw with my other hand, I tilt her head back so she's forced to look at me. Forced to breathe me. "Vlad," she pleads, but it's weak. The blueprints she was holding flutter to the floor at our feet.

Little Irina is anything but weak.

However, I love the idea of overpowering her and bending her to my will.

"Tell me no," I say again, my voice a low, threatening growl.

"No!"

But her body language and eyes scream yes.

She would never willingly betray her sister.

Good thing I have no such loyalty.

I crush my lips to hers, craving her taste more than any

119

fancy scotch or vodka from my expensive stash. I want to taste every delicious inch of her. Her lips are soft and pliable. I easily urge them open with my tongue and invade her mouth. She does taste sweet, like vanilla essence. Her tiny fists pound at my shoulders, but her lips dance with mine. Desperately. Eagerly. Dangerously. Once she realizes she's a victim of my kiss and I'm not letting her go, her body softens against me. I nip, suck, and plunder her mouth, taking my fill.

Goddamn, she tastes like perfection.

I pull away, much to my cock's horror. I could spend hours kissing her sweet, pouty mouth that tastes like sin delivered straight from heaven. An unearthly, divine concoction. She's a meal fit for a king, and I want to devour her.

Our eyes meet for a moment. Hers are glazed over with lust, but she quickly shakes away her daze before glowering at me and muttering a string of Russian curse words. She's unsteady on her feet as she pulls away, but finds her equilibrium and darts out of my office like the devil is chasing her.

I'm the devil all right.

And I want to *chase her*, but if I do, I won't stop with her lips.

I'll devour all of her.

CHAPTER THIRTEEN

Irina

Oh my God.

My heart hasn't stopped racing since this afternoon. Since Vlad held me in his grip and kissed me like our lives depended on it. I was horrified. Horrified and completely turned on.

Guilt claws at me, and I fret as I dig around in my jewelry box looking for something to wear to dinner. I've betrayed my sister in the worst way. What kind of person kisses their sister's fiancé?

Tears threaten, but I blink them away. I've already done too much of that this afternoon. I locked myself in my new room on the other side of the estate once Rada showed me to it and cried for hours. It's not like me to crack and break, but Vlad messes with my head. Some moments I hate him and he disgusts me, then, other moments...I want him so badly, I swear my mouth waters.

I open the bottom drawer of my jewelry box and pull out a dainty tennis bracelet with stones the color of my eyes. It wasn't here before. All my worries are pushed aside as I contemplate where the bracelet came from. Oddly enough, it matches the dress I'd planned to wear for dinner. I slide it on my wrist and admire the stones as they glisten in the overhead light.

"You look beautiful," Diana murmurs from the door-way. She's still dressed in her coat and scarf, her cheeks rosy from the cold.

I can't meet her gaze. Not without my eyes telling her what I did to her. I chew on my lip and stare at the bracelet. "Thanks."

She enters the room as she pulls away her scarf. "Why were you moved here?"

I shrug. "I don't know." My voice trembles, and I hate the sound of it.

"It's a nicer room," she marvels as she sits on the bed. "Shadow, what's wrong?"

"Nothing," I squeak. "How did things go at Father's?"

She lets out a heavy sigh, but doesn't reply. I lift my gaze to find her wringing her scarf in her hands. Dejected. My powerful and charismatic sister is defeated. Her nose turns pink and she regards me with watery eyes.

"I'm sorry," she breathes.

I frown and take a step toward her. "Sorry for what?"

She lets out a humorless laugh. "This." Her hands wave in the air as she sniffles. "Everything."

"It's fine. The Volkov women are strong wherever they are. As long as they're together," I tell her firmly. Whatever happened between Vlad and I will never happen again. I'll make sure of it. I need for this to work for Diana's sake. She's brilliant and successful. Whatever is happening with Father is trying to ruin that. Her alliance with Vlad will only strengthen her.

A tear rolls over her cheek. "He cut us off." She hiccups as more tears stream down.

"I don't have access to any of the accounts."

I rush to sit beside her. The kiss is already a thing of the past and gets swept under the rug as I take my sister's hands. "We'll be fine. You'll marry Vlad and continue doing what you do best. Just for another family. Father will sink without us. We made that company what it is."

She hugs me and cries softly against my hair. "I don't know what our future holds, Shadow. I don't…I just don't know. I never wanted it to come to this. Father is forcing my hand."

"Shhh," I coo. "Today is just a blip, and tomorrow or the next day, he will remember we're the ones who have been there making his companies what they are, especially Volkov Spirits. It will be okay. I promise."

She pulls away and cradles my cheeks in her palms. "I love you, my sweet sister."

Beaming at her, I open my mouth to tell her the words when I notice a bruise on her throat. Not just any bruise. A hickey. My smile drops. "Diana, what is this?"

Her eyes widen, and she looks over her shoulder before trying to cover it with her hand. I slap it away and inspect it closer.

"Who gave you a hickey?" I demand, my eyes wide with horror.

She purses her lips and darts her gaze to the doorway again before jumping from the bed and rushing over to the mirror.

She lets out a breathy curse. "Blyad." *Fuck.*

"Diana?"

"You can't say anything to Vlad," she whispers, coming back to sit by me. "To anyone."

"Tell me," I order.

She swallows and lets out a tortured sigh. "A man. He's older. I've known him for some time."

I blink at her in confusion. "Did he force himself on you?" Vlad will kill him. I'll kill him.

Her nose scrunches. "What? No. We're...we..." she trails off, and more tears roll out. "Shadow, I love him."

No.

This random old man?

Yuck.

"Diana..." I start, my voice low in warning.

She shakes her head. "Stop. I'll hear nothing of it. Your heart can't help who you love, even if it's the wrong person." She lifts her chin. "I won't feel ashamed for what we have."

"What you have?" I hiss. "You can't have anything with him if we're under Vlad's roof and you're to be marrying him. Diana, this is dangerous."

She rises to her feet and snatches up her scarf. "You don't think I know this? You don't think I don't worry every second of every day what it could mean if we get caught?"

"Caught?" I utter. "You've...you've had sex with him?"

She laughs, but it's cold. "Sweet sister, you are so innocent. For that, I am glad. However, you have so much to learn of the outside world." She wraps the scarf around her throat and frowns at me. "I've been sleeping with him for years. Years, Irina. That is love. What we have is love."

My stomach bottoms out at her confession. "Please don't have sex with him here. If Vlad finds out..." I almost gag at the thought of Vlad cutting my sister open like he did his whore. I can't lose her. Vlad isn't the type to take lightly to indiscretions in his own home.

"He almost did find out," she admits, shame in her eyes. "My lover was coming to see me, but Vlad got there first."

"He'll kill you," I whimper. "You have to stop."

She takes a step back as though I've struck her. The strong, powerful woman I know and love has a crazed look in her eyes. Crazed by love. Or...brainwashed. The thought alarms me.

"I'll deal with it," she says finally, lifting her chin. "It will end once I'm married." But the flicker in her eyes tells me otherwise.

"Diana, this isn't you."

She shakes her head. "No," she says, waving all around us, "this isn't me. But we all have our parts to play."

Before I can reply, she hurries from the room.

Vlad may have shoved his tongue down my throat earlier today, but I don't believe for one second he'd take the same thing happening against him lightly. Vlad is a player of an ultimate game where he always comes out the winner. If he noses around and discovers Diana has been sleeping around on him under his own roof, no less, he will want retribution.

That means I need to play my part.

I must distract him.

I head to dinner alone.

Diana was taking forever to get ready and I needed to formulate a plan. She wears another man's mark now. If Vlad sees, he'll lose his mind.

I need to make sure that doesn't happen.

"Ma'am, you look striking this evening," a deep voice murmurs.

I jerk my head to see Stepan leaning against a doorframe,

his suit forming to his body nicely. His eyes rove over the swell of my breasts and then to my bare thighs. Tonight, I opted for a shorter dress. If I plan on distracting Vlad, showing a little leg is in order.

"Thank you," I utter. "Have you seen Mr. Vasiliev?"

"Senior?"

"Uh, no. Vlad."

He shakes his head as he stalks my way, a wolfish gleam in his eyes. I'd once thought he was cute, but now I just want to get away to find Vlad. I have a bigger game to play than hooking a handsome guy. I need to make sure my sister doesn't get herself killed.

Stepan stops inches from me and stares. "Allow me to escort you to dinner."

I step away from him, bumping my ass against the wall. "I...uh..."

"I'll be escorting her to dinner," a cold, masculine voice bites out. "Run along to the basement and check on my Darya."

Stepan stiffens and flashes me a worried look before he steps away, not sparing me a second glance as he storms off. I'm left staring straight into the cold eyes of Yuri Vasiliev. Tall, broad-shouldered, dark hair with streaks of gray—he's an older version of Vlad, handsome and regal. But something in his eyes screams violence. Whatever monster Vlad is, his father is a million times more vile.

"Sir," I greet with a forced smile.

He approaches me, his eyes raking over my dress as he sizes me up. With no expression as to what he thinks, he offers his arm to me. "The dress suits you. Although, I do prefer the one last night over this one."

A flash of memory assaults me.

Shiny and threatening.

A knife.

Not just any knife—Vlad's scary hooked knife.

The small cut on my hip smarts at the thought. I'd wondered what had happened, and now it's all flooding back. Images of Vlad on top of me. Pressed against me. His cock rubbing against my clit through our clothes.

I came.

Dear God, I came.

Heat floods up my throat and paints my flesh what I imagine a brilliant red. Yuri says nothing as he escorts me to the dining room. I'm freaking out over last night when a new feeling surges over me.

Awareness.

Furious rage ripples through the air so palpable, it makes the hairs on my arm stand on end. When I lift my eyes from the floor, I lock gazes with Vlad's enraged amber glare. Everything about his posture and expression states otherwise, but I've learned to read his telling eyes.

His eyes are saying everything to me.

Not saying, screaming.

Get. Away. From. Him.

I start to pull away from Yuri, but his grip tightens.

"Ah, child, not so fast. We're playing a game. Do you like games?" He turns his head and lifts a brow at me.

"What sort of game?" I murmur.

The heat of Vlad's stare burns my flesh. I want to glance over at him again, but I'm snared in Yuri's demanding stare.

"My game. They're all my games, after all." His lips lift on one side. This is the same man who beat the ever-loving snot out of Darya. Did he rape her too?

I straighten my spine and lift my chin. "I don't want to

play games with you."

"Father," Vlad says coolly. I'm surprised he reached us so quickly.

Yuri smiles at him in a polite manner. "Son."

"Allow me to escort Irina to her seat," Vlad growls, his voice slightly on edge. "I insist."

His father chuckles. Low and deadly. "Not tonight, son. She's mine for tonight." He regards me with a devilish grin. "An old man with a young, beautiful woman on his arm for the evening, I can't think of a better way I'd like to spend dinner."

Vlad flashes me a warning glare. Something glimmers in his amber eyes. Fear. I'm struck by the glimpse and nearly stumble when Yuri guides me to the table. He pulls out a chair and motions for me to sit.

I take my seat and guzzle down the water in the goblet. I'll avoid wine. The last thing I need is to lose my head while in Yuri Vasiliev's grip. I saw what he did to Darya. I'll be damned if he does that to me. He doesn't take his seat right away as he talks to Veniamin Vetrov's father, Yegor. Yegor is as old as Yuri but he's not fit like Yuri. Yegor has a giant belly that strains against the buttons of his dress shirt. Yuri is powerful and scary next to Yegor, who is pudgy and breathing too heavily. I notice Veniamin sitting across the table wearing a knowing expression, his narrowed stare on me.

I'm suddenly struck by a horrible realization.

Ven.

My sister is sleeping with Ven.

Older, and she's known him forever. He's always at the Vasiliev home. As if clued into my thoughts, Ven smirks.

Oh God.

I remember being a kid and seeing them kiss in the

hallway of our home. Back when he'd recently grown his beard and attended university, but far too old to be kissing a teenager. I'd been stunned, but Diana never spoke of it again.

Because he was her secret.

Crap!

This will cause a war. If my sister is screwing Ven while engaged to Vlad, that'll put three families at war with each other.

His attention darts to the doorway, and I follow his gaze. Diana enters the dining room wearing a confident smile and a fashionable scarf that goes well with her black dress hugging all her voluptuous curves. I let out a sigh of relief noticing her hickey is hidden. Anton follows behind her, ever the good watch dog. Ven rises and struts over to them, causing my stomach to hollow out. When he reaches her, she flashes him a brilliant grin. He takes her hand and kisses the top of it.

Double crap!

Why would she blatantly flaunt this in front of everyone?

Ven has completely brainwashed my sister.

I start to rise to my feet to stop whatever it is that's happening, but then everyone takes their seats. Ven sits back down across from me as Yuri sits to my left. Vlad sits beside me, and Diana sits across from him with Anton at her left.

My eyes are glued to them as Ven scratches his dark beard, a flirtatious grin on his face as he leans in and whispers something to Diana. She giggles, and it sets my teeth on edge. I can sense Vlad beside me staring them down.

Triple crap!

"Miss Volkov," Yuri says, startling me. "Have you

considered entering the next V Games? You're certainly old enough. Vlad entered when he was much younger than you are now."

Surprised by his words, I jerk my head to the left and gape at him. "W-What? Me?"

He shrugs as a server sets down a steaming plate in front of him. She then serves me and Vlad, who's engaged in conversation with a man beside him, before moving along. I swallow, the scent of baked salmon invading my senses.

"I know about your father. About that bastard son of his he now favors over his daughters. I know everything, dear girl. How you now rely on that of the Vasiliev to secure your future and well-being. Am I incorrect?"

I stiffen, but don't respond. I stare down at the delicious looking salmon and try not to recoil at Yuri's words.

"I could train you…" he mutters lowly.

Jerking my head his way, I glare at him. "Like you trained Darya?"

He smirks, ignoring the bite in my tone. "No, Darya is good for a violent fuck. She screams, and boy, does she scream loud. Those screams will entice even the most focused of fighters." He leans forward and runs the tip of his finger along my outer arm. "But you're way too strong and smart for that. Brilliant girls who can run their daddy's businesses with their eyes closed deserve to be much bigger players than ones who lie on their back with their legs spread open."

"No thank you." I level him with a hard stare.

"We'll see."

I turn away from him and pick up my fork. I'm about to take a bite when I see Diana glaring at Yuri.

"Irina is far too valuable to risk in The Games," she bites

out, overhearing our conversation despite flirting with her lover. "Our father may be smitten at the moment with his newfound son, but he's always been a fickle man. His love for us hasn't changed, and he's always known assets such as us can't be risked on the appetites of the depraved within The Games."

Yuri's eyes flare with fire. His jaw clenches as though he's barely able to keep vicious, uncontrolled words from spewing from his mouth.

Vika bites into a strawberry she's plucked from her champagne flute and asks while chewing, "If you're loved so much by him, then why has he cut you out of his businesses?" The glint in Vika's eyes, like she won a prize, makes me want to jab my fork into one.

How can she possibly know anything of this?

Diana tuts, a smirk on her lips. "Vika, who fills your head with such things? It's true that dynamics have changed, but our father trained us. He prepared us for the cutthroat world and I've been running the business for quite some time. In that time, shares have been moved over into my own name. Volkov Spirits is a company Irina and I built from the ground up. He can have the rest to pass on to Vas, if that's what he chooses, but Volkov Spirits is and will always be ours."

My heart pounds in my chest.

Vika turns a pink color and downs the rest of her drink in one gulp. Just when I think she's going to shut up, she speaks again. "Lots of families send their children into The Games. It's an honor and a sign of strength. For almost a decade, since The Games have been around, it has been this way. Most of the young men sitting at this table, like my brother, entered The Games as a rite of passage into adulthood—into leading their families. Are you saying your family is better than the rest of us? Why? Because you're a woman?"

She's such a bitch. Why does she always have to create conflict?

"I'm not saying that at all," Diana replies with a lift of her chin. "I'm saying *we* don't need to prove our worth that way. Female or not."

"She's a businesswoman. I like it," Ven says with a grin, playfully tugging at Diana's scarf. Their blatant flirting is going to get her killed by the time the night's over. Before I lose my nerve, I do something I can't take back:

I make my move.

CHAPTER FOURTEEN

Vlad

My attention is wavering from the scene before me as Arkady Orlov drones on beside me about a new cocaine supplier. The Orlovs are the biggest drug runners on this side of Russia. I've been wanting to steal a piece of their market and have been watching them closely.

Except now.

Now I'm watching my fiancée and Ven making a fool of the Vasiliev name as they practically play grab-ass at the dining room table in front of everyone. I accused her of it, but it's looking apparent that he's fucking her.

All thoughts of the Orlovs and cocaine and murder dissipate when a foot nudges mine. At first, I think Irina accidentally touched my foot, but when I look over at her, her cheeks are pink as she does it again. A bare foot slides up my ankle and playfully rubs against the side of my leg. My cock responds with a jolt.

"Irina," I growl under my breath.

She looks up at me from under her heavily darkened with mascara lashes and smiles. So damn innocent. A little angel flirting with the devil. Naughty girl. Naughty, naughty girl. "I want to paint you."

I stare at her in confusion. In one simple sentence, she's rocked my entire world. I find my mask slipping as I indulge this little princess. "Oh?"

She nods, tucking a blonde strand of hair behind her ear. Her toes continue to playfully tease me under the table and my cock strains in my slacks. It may as well just be she and I in this room. Nobody else matters. Not Diana. Not the marriage. Not the Vasiliev name or my awful father.

Just Shadow, brilliant like the sun.

"Why?" I ask, curious of her sudden flirtations.

She shrugs. "Because you're something beautiful. I like to paint beautiful things." I don't sense deception in her words. Just honest to God truth.

"Perhaps one day," I tell her, turning my head toward the sound of Diana's laughter.

A slender leg hooks over mine under the tablecloth and I jerk my head back to Irina. Her icy blue eyes blaze with determination. Full, pouty lips that have been painted a seductive red part and entice me. Those lips were mine this afternoon. I owned and teased them. I'll have them again. Knowing she's spread open under the table drives me mad with need. Slipping my hand under the cloth, I palm her bare thigh above her knee hooked over my leg. She shivers, but doesn't pull away.

"Why the sudden change of heart?" I ask as I take a bite of salmon with my free hand.

She mimics my action and gasps slightly when I caress her silky flesh. "I have needs," she states bluntly.

I chew slowly and stare her down. She's gorgeous tonight in a demure but short black dress that showcases what a knockout she is. I nearly came unglued seeing her at my father's side earlier. If it wouldn't have caused a scene, I would have plucked her from his grip and tossed her over my shoulder like a goddamn caveman. I'm still tempted to do just that.

"I could see to those needs," I murmur, my hand slowly sliding up her naked thigh.

Her breath hitches and she trembles. "Vlad." The needy whine of her voice has me blind with lust. I've never wanted something so bad in my entire life.

I am going to fuck sweet little Irina. The idea of it almost steals the air from my lungs. I told myself no. Committed myself to the idea of marrying Diana and not taking what I really want. But after sitting through a dinner of Diana laughing and touching Ven every few seconds, I've decided I don't owe her a goddamn thing, and what she doesn't know can't hurt her anyway. Right?

Oh, sweet, little Irina will come for me. She will spread her milky thighs and I'll explore the treasures no man has ever seen or touched before. Then, maybe it will get her out my system and I can move on and become the husband I'm designated to be to her sister.

Don't worry, Shadow, you will get what you so desperately crave.

That's matter of fact.

She must know this by now.

It's happening.

"Your sister is watching," I taunt, gaging her for a reaction.

Her brows furrow and she quickly looks over at Diana. She smiles at her sister until I slip my palm higher up her thigh, stealing that smile right from her face.

Dinner continues, and I keep my palm firmly attached to her. I bet her panties are dripping with excitement. I'm craving to taste her arousal.

As soon as she finishes, she touches my bicep. "I'd like

to paint you." Fire blazes in her gaze. "Now."

I lift a brow in question. "Now?"

"Now," she repeats.

"Paint?" Father inquires from beside her.

"A wedding gift for Diana," Irina says flawlessly, the lie unnoticeable to anyone but me. She untangles herself from me and stands. "Excuse me."

"Your studio isn't ready," I tell her, "but I know of a place."

I rise and offer my father a nod. Diana is too engrossed in what Ven is saying to notice I'm leaving to put my dick inside her sister. Irina rushes from the dining room, her black dress bouncing around her. I stalk her like she's my prey. As soon as she enters the hallway, she pulls off her shoes and takes off in a sprint. It takes a moment for my mind to catch up with the fact that she's running from me.

The chase is always my favorite part.

I'll catch her.

I don't waste any time and charge after her. It may be goddamn cold in Russia, but I still put at least eight miles a day running on a treadmill. Indoors. Where it's warm. She'll never outrun me. I hear a door slam. She's gone into my father's wing of the house. My sweet little Irina is lucky I'm here to protect her. Left alone in Daddy's lair is an awful place to be.

I push open the door to Father's sitting room and find her with her back against a bookcase. Kicking the door behind me, I prowl her way. Her blue eyes are wide and frightened, making my heart race with excitement.

"Vlad," she starts, her voice hoarse and terrified.

"Shhh." I stalk over to her and grasp her delicate neck in my hand—the same hand that was up her dress earlier. Her shoes fall to the wood floor with a clatter. "You can't tease a lion and not expect to get eaten."

She cries out when I pin her to the bookshelf and attack her mouth with mine. My thumb strokes the side of her neck, reveling in the way her pulse goes wild beneath my touch. At first, her kiss is clumsy and unsure, but then she's clawing at the lapels of my jacket. I abandon my grip on her throat to touch her in other places. My palms skim along her ribs, then slide around to her ass. I lift her and groan when she spreads her slender legs to allow me where we both know I need to be.

My cock is painfully hard, and I grind against her soft center as I nip at her bottom lip. Her moan is needy. A sweet beg. "Do you remember last night now?"

She moans again. "Yes."

"Your body is so receptive. You want this, Irina. You want me to destroy every part of you. You'll love it."

She nods, sliding her fingers into my hair. Her grip tightens around my thick locks as she deepens our kiss. We both fight desperately to have the upper hand, and hell if she isn't winning. I'm consumed by the need to have her. I buck against her, eager to see her come apart again because of me. The little bad girl loses control and rocks with me in anticipation of her release. I pull a hand from her perfect ass to grip her perky tit through her dress. The sounds coming from her are wild and crazed.

"I'm going to fuck you," I snarl, my teeth nipping her lip, then chin. She cries out when I bite her throat. I move my mouth near her ear and nibble the skin there as well. "I'm going to fuck you right here against my father's books."

She whimpers, my words sending her over the edge. Her body shatters with an orgasm. If she comes so easily just from a little rubbing, I can't wait to watch her lose her mind when I use my tongue.

Before she comes down from her high, I slide my hand between us and find her panties. Wet. Soaked. She's so hot for me, she's making a mess. It makes me fucking crazy. I slide her panties to the side, and a choked sound escapes her.

"Vlad…I…this isn't…I'm…we can't do this."

I yank at my belt, then unfasten my slacks. She's gasping and writhing, but not trying to get away. When I free my thick, aching cock and rub it against her clit, she jolts in my grip. "Then tell me no," I beg, my mouth a whisper over hers.

"Vlad…" she moans. "No, please." Her whines are needy. She says what her heart screams at her to say so she won't betray her sister, but her body begs for the opposite.

She wants me to be the bad guy.

It's a good damn thing I enjoy the hell out of that notion.

"No turning back now, little shadow," I threaten, my teeth nipping at her swollen lip. "You started this, and now, you'll finish it."

Her fingers scratch through my scalp and she nods, but she whispers the words, "No, we can't."

"Of course we can," I growl. "And we will."

I kiss her mouth to muffle her screams as I slide my tip to her tight opening and impale her with a quick, violent thrust that has books falling off the shelf beside us.

Tight.

Fuck, my sweet little virgin is tight.

Her cunt suffocates my cock. It's her pussy that is the sadist, not me. It's the one into choking at the moment, and all I can do is let her slowly kill me with pleasure. She's the best damn thing I've ever sunk my dick into.

"OW!" she cries out, her fingers ripping at my hair. "We can't do this." Her words are breathy as her hands tug at me, bringing me closer, contradicting the words slipping off her tongue.

It's cute, the battle of what her heart begs and body dictates.

I slowly pull out, then slam into her again. A loud, ugly sob rips from her, so I silence her with another kiss. One's virginity loss is never a pleasurable event. At least not for the woman. She'll hurt for days after as she remembers how I took over her body from the inside out. Like the devil himself sent to invade her soul.

"Vlad," she cries, "please." She whimpers. "We can't"

"But we are," I remind her, pounding harder into her, driving home my point.

I fuck her hard and fast, kissing her perfect mouth.

"Vlad," she pleads again. "Oh God."

"I know, little one. I know. Let me own you."

Her grip on my hair lessens and she slides her palms to the outside of my neck. She relaxes some, and my chest fills with pride that she trusts me to take care of her. I rock my hips into her, making sure to grind against her sensitive clit with each thrust. Her cunt is dripping from her last orgasm, giving me all the lubrication I need to slide in and out easily. She goes from trying to get away to clinging to me as though I'm a life raft.

"Vlad…"

"So perfect," I breathe against her mouth. "So mine."

Her body trembles and quakes, but I know she won't come like this. Not her first time. So, I fuck her hard and good. Soon, I'll take hours drawing pleasure from her.

When she can thoroughly enjoy it without pain.

And then…

Then I'll bring her into my dark world where pain is the king over pleasure. He rules with an iron fist. And pleasure bends to the will of pain. I will show her my kingdom. She will be my queen.

I grunt as my nuts seize up with my orgasm. It's a major test to my willpower, but I manage to slip out of her as I spurt my seed against her lower stomach. We're both breathing heavily, and she clutches onto me as though she never wants to let go.

Because of those in our world, she'll be forced to let go and soon.

But right here, in this room, she can have me. All of me. *The real me.*

I nuzzle my nose along hers, then lean my forehead against hers. "Irina."

"Vlad," she whispers.

"You're dangerous to me," I admit, my voice hoarse and husky.

"You'll survive," she teases.

Pulling away, I stare into her glimmering eyes. A heavy emotion shines in them—one I've seen surface over the years when she looks my way. One that was stronger this afternoon when we kissed. A look that now nearly knocks me over.

Falling.

She's falling so hard.

I'll catch her.

"Nobody can know." I hate having to ruin this moment with the truth.

Her lip trembles. *"I know."*

"As do I. We're the *only* ones who know."

I pull away and set her to her feet. Her entire body shakes as her dress falls into place, my cum creating a wet spot where her stomach is. It speaks to my inner animal. Possessive, crushing thoughts overwhelm me.

Fucking mine.

The little sun named Shadow is mine.

"Vlad?" Her voice is soft and unsure.

"Yes, solntce moyo?"

She regards me with a soft expression. "I still want to paint you."

My chest cracks open, and I let this girl in. I know it's foolish. Everyone I let in either dies or betrays me or leaves me. And yet...

"You will," I assure her. "Let's get to it. I'm not done with you yet."

I don't think I'll ever be done with her.

The events of the day wear on me and I find myself drifting to sleep in the armchair in Irina's new room. She's been in her bathroom for what feels like forever. I fall sleep until her soft voice awakens me.

"Vlad?"

"Mmm?"

"Can you lose the jacket?"

I blink open my eyes to find her sitting on the floor in front of me. Her easels must be still packed away, but I can see where she's dragged out items from bags and spread them around her. Paints and brushes. A blank canvas. Her wet hair is twisted into a messy bun and her face is free of makeup. Freckles that are usually hidden by makeup make their appearance, reminding me of when she was younger.

"You're beautiful," I murmur.

She smiles at me. "Thank you. Now get naked."

"Naked?" I chuckle at her boldness, but rise to my feet. She's so damn cute in a black tank top and tight, black yoga pants. Her feet are bare and I have the urge to kiss them. Never in my life have I wanted to kiss someone's feet. But with her little painted toes wiggling, I'm thinking kissing her feet sounds entirely too enticing.

Pulling off my jacket, I drape it over the back of my chair. Her brows are furrowed as she watches me. I pluck through the buttons of my vest and lose it along with my tie. I slowly undo my dress shirt, enjoying the hungry way she's watching me.

"How's your cunt?" I ask.

Her cheeks burn bright red. "Fine."

I chuckle and slide the shirt off my shoulders. When I tug off the wife beater, I regard her with a lifted brow. "Want me to keep going?"

She swallows and nods. "I know what I want to paint. Keep going."

Amused, I unbuckle my belt and send my slacks to the floor, kicking out of them and my shoes. She points at my socks, and I laugh. When I start to pull off my black boxer briefs, she stops me.

"Leave those on and sit back down. You can go back to sleep if you want." Her embarrassment fades as she busies herself with her paints.

"I was just sure you wanted to paint my dick," I tease.

She lets out a cute laugh. "Typical male. It's not all

about the penis. It's about the male form." Her skin flushes. "Not just any male. You."

I settle into the chair and sprawl my legs out. Seeing her look so damn adorable in her element has my cock hardening again.

"Hey now," she says playfully, "keep that thing in check. I have a man to paint."

I chuckle. It's real and uncharacteristic for me. She makes me feel free, unburdened, and young. She makes me feel like a man and a boy all in one. I've never felt so relaxed around another person before. I've taken my clothes off, but she makes me feel naked. Like I'm baring not just my skin and body, but also my soul.

I scratch at the side of my jaw as I stare at her. She's beautiful when she paints. Her eyes seem to glaze over as she sees parts of the world nobody else sees. I find myself enraptured in her stare. After a while of her quietly painting, I start to drift off again.

"Vlad?"

"Mmm?" I don't open my eyes.

"Keep doing what you're doing."

What *am* I doing?

The sounds of her light breathing lull me to sleep and dreams of her bombard me as I drift deeper into the unknown. This thing between us won't last—it can't—but I want it to. With all that I am.

Keep doing what I'm doing?

That shouldn't be a problem.

Even if I have to keep *doing* it in secret.

CHAPTER FIFTEEN

Irina

I wake buried under a mountain of covers. A yawn steals over me as I push the blankets away and squint at the morning sun. I look over at the chair in my room, but Vlad is no longer there. Vaguely, I remember him carrying me to bed after I fell asleep.

Everything hurts.

I feel bruised and used.

But I also feel good too.

My pussy hurts, but triumph surges through me. I did it. I managed to distract and get the great Vlad Vasiliev to fuck me so he won't kill my sister. Easy. I'm a genius.

Except now, I feel like I've made things ten times more complicated. Sure, I allowed my sister to sleep with Ven without interruption by distracting her fiancé into taking my virginity, and if that isn't screwed up, I don't know what is.

I slide out of my bed and rush over to my painting. It's crude and messy, but I love it. Vlad, asleep and vulnerable. I've never seen anything more beautiful, except the real thing, of course. I could stare at him like this for hours.

Bang! Bang! Bang!

"Irina," Diana calls out on the other side of the door. It's then I realize it's closed and locked. I didn't panic. I felt safe last night. The thought is surprising, and I tuck it away to ponder later.

"Coming!" I shove the canvas under the bed and rush over to the door.

When I open it, she is a picture of perfection. She no longer wears a scarf, but she's covered her love bite with makeup. "Good morning, lazy buns. Do you know what time it is?"

I shrug. "No. Why?"

"It's just not like you to sleep the day away. Especially with all that banging going on down the hall." She sighs as she regards me. "Thank you."

I lift my brows. "For what?"

"For distracting Vlad. I knew you were trying to protect me. I've been careless, and I'm sorry you felt you needed to pick up the slack. Thanks for distracting him." She looks around and eyes the paints on the floor. "Yuri said you were painting Vlad for me. Where's the painting?"

"Uh, he took it. You can't see your wedding gift early," I say in exasperation. I quickly change the subject. "Did you...?"

She blinks slowly and smiles. "We took the stolen opportunity, yes. Made love, and then I sent him away from my room before anyone would notice." She toys with a lock of messy hair that's fallen loose from my bun. "One day, you'll understand what it feels like to have sex. It's unlike anything you'll ever experience."

Oh, do I know...

"Sounds interesting," I murmur.

"It hurts at first," she tells me, her brows furling. "My first time, I cried. A lot." She shudders, and for a brief moment, my sister looks haggard. Broken and depressed. I hate the look on her. This is not my Diana. "But you grow to love it. It's like they get inside your mind and live there. They say all the right things that sing to your heart." She sighs. "Love is painful sometimes."

"Diana," I start, but the words fall short. "I just want you to be happy."

Her nostrils flare, and she frowns. "Happiness isn't with Vlad Vasiliev. I knew this when I agreed to marry him." I note the bitterness in her tone. It's so strange to me because I feel the opposite. Last night, Vlad uncovered a new part of me. Those hours after we had sex and I painted him, I felt closer to him than I ever felt toward anyone. Even Diana.

"I think happiness can be found with Vlad," I murmur, my words more for me than her.

"You've much to learn, Shadow." She kisses me on the head and starts for the door. "I want to meet later. We have to make a new game plan now that Father has made a mess of things."

"Of course. We'll figure it out," I assure her.

She smiles, but it doesn't reach her eyes, and then she's gone. As soon as she leaves, I walk into the bathroom and look at my reflection. I'm a terrible person. Lying to my sister. Fucking her fiancé behind her back. Ugh. I peel off my tank top. Maybe a shower will cleanse away this dirty feeling. When I notice the paint across my abdomen, I gasp.

Mine.

Black paint.

Neat, precise writing.

I run my fingers across the letters and can't fight the smile on my lips. This game Vlad and I are playing…I like it. I like it a lot.

Unlike at the recent V Games, I just hope a Volkov

doesn't lose to a Vasiliev.

Something tells me silly, hopeful girls shouldn't be playing with violent, masterful men.

Perhaps in some games there are two winners…

I clench my thighs and wince at the lingering pain.

Perhaps not.

There's a different atmosphere around here today. But I'm not sure if it's just that I feel different—more like a woman, yet the giddy feeling of being a girl as well. It's different. I walk into the kitchen to find Vika and Vlad in a heated discussion. Diana is standing close by with her arms folded across her chest and a look of annoyance on her pretty pursed lips.

"What's going on?" I ask her in a hushed tone, budging up next to her.

"Vika being a petulant child as usual," she hisses.

I drag my eyes back over to the two of them. Vlad's pulse ticks in his neck and his jaw is clenched. His eyes are fire and brimstone as he peers down at his sister. She appears to realize she's poking a tiger in his own cage and deflates.

"Fine," she concedes with an exasperated huff. "I'll go. Diana can accompany me." She turns her sickly smile in our direction, and Diana smiles tightly back at her. "We are going to be sisters, after all."

"Of course, I'd love to help pick out your dress," Diana says sweetly. "Maybe I can shop for my own while we're there."

Images of Diana wearing a wedding dress standing

beside Vlad conjure up in my mind and I wilt inside. A dying flower starved of light. She will be a beautiful bride.

"It's a long trip, so pack an overnight bag," Vika tells Diana on her way out of the kitchen, tossing her scarf over her shoulder and whipping me in the face with it. Bitch.

"Perfect," Diana huffs out, following Vika's exit.

I watch the door close softly behind her, then turn my gaze on Vlad, who is staring back at me, a fierce hunger in his eyes.

We're alone.

Being alone with him makes my skin heat and my body burn from the inside out.

"How did you sleep?" he asks, the rasp in his throat signaling the equal effect I have on him. My head swims and heat spreads throughout my stomach, pooling in my core.

"Fine, thank you," I squeak out, my nerves rattling me. "Sheesh, I'm starving. Would you like some breakfast? Can I fix you something?" I escape his nearness and hurry over to the fridge. My legs feel heavy, like I'm dragging lead weights across the room.

His shoes squeak across the tile behind me, signaling his approach. "It's noon, Irina," he says lowly, a husky growl rumbling through him. "But yes, I could eat." With that, he blocks the way between me and the refrigerator, grasps me under the arms, and sits me on the edge of the counter.

"Vlad!" I whisper-yell, placing my hands on his shoulders to push him away. His strength is no match for me. He forces my legs to part and wedges himself between them. "Diana could come back!" I say desperately.

Ignoring my worry, he slaps the counter on either side of my legs. "Lie back," he instructs. When I gape at him, he pushes my dress up my thighs and starts tugging down my panties. Wearing dresses has never been my thing, but I must say, they've been awfully convenient lately. I take back everything negative I ever thought about them.

My heart hammers inside my chest and my head swims with need, fear, and excitement all rolled into one. He lifts my feet and places them on the edge of the counter, opening me up for his eyes to devour. My panties get shoved into his pocket for safekeeping. Embarrassment washes through me, but it's replaced with a groan when he dips his head and kisses me between my thighs. I gasp and collapse back onto the counter, the cold surface penetrating my fevered flesh through the fabric of my dress.

Oh God.

His greedy mouth. His hot, slick tongue. His powerful, wandering hands.

Too much.

He feasts on me, like I'm a buffet laid out just for him. And I am. Just. For. Him. Warm laps of his tongue travel the length of my lips, separating them and finding the throbbing clit hidden away inside.

I grasp the side of the counter to ground myself. I feel like I'm floating away on a cloud of ecstasy. Do all men do this? Does it always feel this good?

My back arches as he sucks my clit into his mouth. I feel a swirling building in my stomach and heat spreading throughout my body in waves. Something prods at my opening, and then I'm filled with what I believe to be his finger. It hurts and pleasures in the same breath. I'm flying. I'm going to come undone right here on the kitchen counter.

I startle when the kitchen door opens and a male voice chokes out, "Blyad, prostite, gospodin." *Fuck, sorry, sir.*

I hurry to sit up and frantically push my dress down to hide what we've been doing. Vlad stares at me wolfishly, a sheen of my juices coating his mouth.

He's the hunter and I'm the prey.

Vlad murmurs an order meant for only me to hear. "Zakroy svoi glaza, solntce moyo." *Close your eyes, my sun.*

My insides cramp with worry and I can't do as he asks. Instead, I watch in guilt-ridden horror as he prowls toward the man who backs up knowing he's walked into something he won't walk out of.

"Vlad," he pleads, but Vlad is quick, silent, and as deadly as they come. His arm snaps out, landing a closed fist to the man's throat. The man gasps in shock and grasps at his larynx, making a wheezing sound. His eyes are wide and panicked. Vlad rounds him, slipping something from his pocket and clasping an arm around the man, putting him in a headlock.

Fast, efficient jabs to the neck, the object shines when the light catches it. It's a knife. Not the fish hook one. A different one—one with their crest etched into it. The imperial two-headed eagle. The man sags in his arms, blood spurting from the wounds in his neck.

Normally unemotional, calm eyes blaze with wildness. Vlad's expression is crazed for a moment before he blinks it away and releases the man. He falls to the floor with a thud, blood puddling around him.

I stare for a second until I think I'll be sick. Bile races up my throat, and I jump down from the counter to rush to the sink. I retch, and tears spring to my eyes. I've seen men killed before—hell, even women, by Vlad's hand, no less—but this was not because of something they did. It was for something we did. I did. He was protecting us—the awful things we were doing. That means I'm a monster too.

"Irina," Vlad says, his voice quiet and collected. Fingers run down my spine, offering me comfort. "He has a loose tongue. He would have talked." He continues to stroke me, and I wonder if he's smearing blood all over my clothes.

I shudder and nod, wiping a hand across my mouth. "I know," I tell him, because I do. I quickly wash my hands, but it doesn't clean away the dirtiness I feel all over right now.

"Go help Diana pack for tonight," he urges, his tone soft and gentle. It's hard to come to terms with who's touching me and who stabbed a man to death seconds ago. "I'll have food brought to you when I've cleaned this mess up."

"Okay," I manage, then pull away from the sink to leave, my body trembling violently.

His hand grasps mine before I get too far away. The heat and comfort he provides with his strong touch grounds me. The shaking subsides as his fingers trace over my palm. He stares at me, his eyes making promises I somehow understand down to a cellular level.

What's happening between us is unstoppable.

An arranged marriage. His bratty, meddling sister. A potential loose-lipped man.

Nothing will snuff out what has begun to rage between us. An inferno. A fiery explosion of epic proportions.

We are the sun.

This isn't just lust taking us over. This is so much more. Something that needs to be protected and kept from everyone else.

Our fingers dance with each other's before our connection breaks. With watery eyes, but a new resolve, I push out the doors and allow him to do what he does best.

Take control. Handle things. Make moves that ensure he wins.

And this time, I hope he does win, because we're on the same team.

CHAPTER SIXTEEN

Vlad

Stepan enters the kitchen five minutes after I called him. He looks down at one of my father's lackeys and raises a questioning brow. It's not his job to question me, so I ignore his unspoken request and tell him to take care of it.

Leaving him to it, I make my way to my office. I was rash and foolish to take Irina like that in the open, but seeing her flushed from sleep and knowing my scent would be lingering on her skin from last night was too tempting. There were so many things I wanted to do to her I didn't get time for last night, my urges overtook me, and for once, I let them.

I slip behind my desk and bring up the camera monitors for the kitchen. I rewind the feed and delete the recorded indiscretion. Problem solved.

Sighing, I lean back in the chair and relish her flavor still lingering on my lips. She consumes me. Now that I've tasted her, I don't think I can ever stop.

She's mine.

And that's not changing any time soon.

Diana knocks on the office door, but before she can enter, she is shoved aside as Vika waltzes in.

"Diana's servant is going to drive us," she whips out,

checking her nails. "Does Father know you're already making me pick out my dress?" Her snide tone makes me want to laugh, but I don't.

"Father doesn't care, Vika," I tell her, emotionless. Bored even. I'm already so goddamn bored with her. "Why should he?"

She spits more venom before turning on her heel. "Ya nenaviju tebya." *I hate you.*

"He's not a servant," Diana informs her as she passes.

"What?" Vika snaps.

"Anton," Diana says coolly. "He's a bodyguard, not a servant."

Rolling her eyes, Vika flees the room, leaving Diana and I alone.

Diana walks toward me and stops next to a picture of Viktor and I. It's the same one Irina was playing with when she was in here. She picks it up and studies it. "With Viktor's death, I thought you'd have gotten closer, but you appear to be at odds with your sister."

I stand and round the table, taking the picture from her hand and placing it down. "Vika has always had her own agenda. She doesn't care about Viktor."

Her brows furl as she places a hand over my heart. "You speak of him like he's still here."

"I still feel him here," I tell her honestly.

"Maybe you shouldn't have allowed him to enter The Games," she adds brazenly.

I study her features for a moment. This woman is supposed to be my wife soon. Irritation bubbles up inside me. Sometimes I wonder if Diana and I are too similar to be properly matched. One day, her tendency to question my authority will rub me the wrong way and it won't end pretty.

"Are you saying I didn't value my brother's life like you do Irina's?" I attempt to keep my voice steady, but anger causes it to shake slightly. She is walking on thin ice. Viktor is a trigger for my less calm side.

She drops her hand and shrugs a shoulder. "I'm just saying I would have never risked Irina like that."

"You know our life," I spit out. "Viktor lived to enter The Games. He wanted to prove himself to my father."

"Well, it didn't work," she says with a huff. "Did it?"

Anger coils my nerves. How dare she speak of things she doesn't understand?

"Shagay ostorojno, Diana." *Tread carefully, Diana.*

Her lips purse and she gives me a slight nod. She knows she's pushed as far as she can for one day. I'm seconds from snapping. "I'll be back tomorrow," she says, her voice all business as she changes the subject. "Irina is taking a nap. She's exhausted for some reason. Please make sure she eats some dinner."

"I will."

She stands on her tiptoes and plants a chaste kiss to my cheek. "Vlad." With that, she walks toward the door.

"Safe travels," I call out to her retreating form. She doesn't say another word as she leaves.

I take a seat back at my desk and smile at the idea of sweet little Irina needing to nap. Smooth, creamy skin on display. A soft pout on her supple lips as she sleeps. Gorgeous blonde hair in disarray. My cock is getting hard just thinking about pulling away her covers to view the delectable woman who would no doubt be hiding beneath.

All warmth is sucked from the room as a chill rattles down my spine. My back straightens when my father enters my office. He hardly ever comes here. If he wants me, he summons me, and like the loyal son I am, I obey.

"Otets?" It comes out as a question more than a greeting. I start to stand, but he holds his hand up to stop me.

"Sit," he orders. He pours himself a drink from the canter I keep on my desk. Taking his time to get to the point is another of Father's favorite games. To keep people on edge and waiting. But knowing this already, I simply wait him out. Two can play at his game. He's no longer the ruler in my world, despite what he may think.

"Ruslan's birthday is next month," he says finally. "Let's throw him a party and announce the marriage date. I want this marriage settled right away."

Perfect. The sooner the better.

"Sounds like a great idea," I concur. His shoulders are squared as he sips his vodka—a new brand, compliments of my fiancée. Evidently, Father is not done speaking.

"I want Darya brought into the main house and given living quarters." His amber eyes narrow as he pins me with a hard stare, daring me to disagree.

I bite back a smirk and lean forward, clasping my hands together in front of me on the desk. "Oh?"

He's never taken an interest in one of his fuck toys.

As if appearing to ponder this choice, he frowns for a moment before settling with a slight nod. He downs the contents of his glass and sets it down loudly. "She reminds me of your mother. I think I'll keep her around for a month or two."

My heart picks up speed at the mention of my mother. He never talks of her. She left when I was young, and we've never seen her since. Father won't even keep pictures of her around. She scorned him, created an animal in her wake. He's brutal with women, never to keep one around for long, and to have a whore brought into the main house is unheard of. For any of us. But that doesn't mean I'll be the one to tell dear old Dad no. If anything, it reveals a weakness—a weakness I'll enjoy poking and prodding simply to see the effects of it.

"I'll have it seen to," I assure him, though it wasn't a request.

"The youngest Volkov girl?" he asks, and a fire ignites within me.

It takes everything in me not to scowl at the mention of her on his vile tongue. "Irina? What of her?"

He eyes me, studying my features for a moment. I know what he's doing. He's been doing it since I was old enough to speak. Father watches for small tells and then flays you apart with his tongue and his vicious words. He won't find any tells written on my features, though. He schooled me in aloofness many years ago. I learned from the best.

"I'm thinking she may have been a better match for you," he utters, his brows wrinkling together as he considers his words.

What?

An unusual sensation flourishes within me.

Hope?

Goddammit, what sort of game is he playing?

He continues without me forming a response. "Diana is a beautiful girl, but too headstrong. She will need to be reined in, Vlad. Bring her to her knees and show her women may have run the show in the Volkov household, but she will be a Vasiliev soon and we breed men. She will breed sons for you, not run a business she thinks she will still own once that wedding ring is on her finger."

"She will know her place, Father," I all but growl out.

"Don't you worry about these things. I am my father's son, after all." I flash him a dark look.

He grins over at me and runs a hand over his smooth jaw. "Ven appears smitten with the Volkov women. I think Leonid would encourage that coupling."

Thud.

My hands clench, the veins in my arms ready to burst open and paint my desk red. "Irina has forsaken her father," I say calmly. "I doubt she cares what he wants." I sit back, playing indifferent despite the raging anger inside me.

"This is the problem when you raise women to think for themselves," he snarls. He drums his fingers on the arm of the chair. "Maybe this can work in our favor."

"How so?"

I wish he would shut the hell up.

Irina is mine.

Fucking mine.

"We can push her in the direction of who would serve our interests." He's cunning. It's where Vika gets her sly ways.

"Diana won't allow us to decide her sister's fate," I inform him. I won't allow him to send her over to the goddamn vultures.

His face screws up into a sneer. "Diana will do what the hell she's told," he snaps. "You'll set her straight, Vlad, or I'll do it for you." With that, he leans forward like Hades himself looking down on his subjects. "Irina is perfect dick bait for some foolish man. We will use her to trap a Voskoboynikov, perhaps." He smirks, rising to his feet. "For now, let's get Vika married to a Vetrov and be done with her moping around my office hoping I'll change my mind."

He's insane if he thinks I'll allow Ven or a Voskoboynikov

to get anywhere near my sweet Irina.

"Maybe Irina will consider my suggestion for her to enter The Games. A Volkov heir has not proven themselves in The Games yet, and Leonid has expressed interest on investing more money and getting his name into the inner circle. Let him prove his commitment."

"There's a son for that now," I remind him.

He snorts. "There's no honor in that diluted blood. He's a maid's son. The only *honor* he brings is dis*honor*." With that, he leaves me alone to ponder everything he just laid on me.

The need to claim Irina burns through my groin. The moment Father is far from my office, I race up the stairs, two at a time, and discover her door is open and she's lying asleep on the bed for anyone to see.

I prowl into the room and slam the door closed behind me. She startles awake and her eyes expand. Just like I envisioned, her blonde hair is messy, and her lips swollen. Her fist rubs at her eyes as she squints at me. "Vlad, what is it?"

"Take off your clothes," I demand, my tone low and deadly.

She pulls the covers up to her chest, biting on that succulent fat bottom lip, and shakes her head no. "Diana is going to look at wedding dresses, Vlad. I can't do this again. It's wrong."

I stalk toward her, loosening my tie and slipping my jacket from my shoulders along the way. I sling my jacket on the chair I slept in last night. She watches my every move with wide, glimmering blue eyes. I love her stare on me. I want every part of her on me. Reaching out, I snag the covers, jerk them away from her body, and toss them on the floor behind me. She rushes away on all fours, scurrying across the bed like a frightened animal trying to escape a predator.

There is no escape.

I will always capture her.

Grasping her ankle, I tug her backwards, forcing her to collapse to her stomach. I wrap the tie around her ankle and shackle her to the bedpost.

"Vlad, release me," she demands, and it brings a smile to my lips.

"No."

"I'll scream," she threatens.

"I hope so," I tease.

Ripping at her clothes, I tear them from her body. She squeals and fights me, trying to cover herself, but it's futile. She's still pantiless from earlier. I forgot I'd stuffed them in my slacks' pocket. I pull them free and hold them between my teeth while I rip my shirt open and drop it to the floor along with my slacks.

Her body is trembling all over and the wet arousal shows on the inner thighs. She's desperate, just like me. I creep my way over her body and rest my cock between her ass cheeks. My chest brushes against her back and I keep myself from crushing her with my elbows.

"I can't do this." Her voice is soft and lacks conviction as she peers shyly over her shoulder at me.

"Then don't."

Her ass clenches. She's just as hungry for me as I am her. Sweet Irina doesn't want to be bad, but her body didn't get the memo.

"Vlad..." It's a breathy moan as I grind into her ass, spreading her cheeks and resting my cock against her forbidden places.

"If I tell you no and mean it, will you listen?" she asks, but her voice is shaking with need.

"Of course," I lie.

"Then n—" Before she can finish, I stuff her own underwear in her mouth, cutting her off and sending a ripple of pleasure through my own body. She mumbles through the fabric and reaches for them, so I grasp her hands and straddle her, pinning them behind her, resting just above the dimples on her lower back.

"Shhh," I whisper, nibbling her earlobe, then kissing down her shoulder. My lips find their way to her spine. Her body relaxes beneath my lips and I smile knowing I've won. I loosen her hands and bite her ass cheek as I pass it. Forcing her to her knees, I admire her cute ass and pink cunt that's now on display. I use my finger to swipe down her center. She's sopping wet and moans under my touch. Her ass wriggles and squirms, and I can't stand it any longer.

I need to be inside her.

Owning her.

I dip a finger inside, then another, stretching her walls. I slip them out and into my mouth. Her arousal is potent and delicious as it washes over my tongue. I pull her hips toward the end of the mattress and line my cock up to her entrance.

"I know you want this," I murmur, my tip teasing her wet slit. "You won't admit it, but your body tells me everything I need to know."

I enter her, brutal and fast. She groans around the panties as her body rocks against mine, equally desperate for the connection. I buck my hips into her, my skin slapping hers. Her cunt strangles me, begging for more.

I'll give her more.

I'll give her everything.

I squeeze her ass cheek with my hand hard enough to bruise her before pulling it to the side, baring her to me. My thumb strokes against her asshole and I press it past the tight ring just so.

I want her in every possible way.

Ass.

Mouth.

Everything.

Mine.

I slide out of her and relish her whine. Leaning forward, I lick up her ass crease, plundering the tight little hole with my tongue. Her body hums and vibrates as pleasure washes through her. I taste her until she's quivering, just on the edge of bliss.

Goddamn, I can't get enough of her.

I untie her ankle and flip her over. A perfect flush of red is painted all over her skin. Her blazing blue eyes meet mine. Reaching forward, I tug her panties from her mouth and toss them away. She bites on her lip and gives me such a needy look, I have the urge to spill my seed.

She's so damn beautiful.

"Put my cock in your mouth, my little sun," I murmur, my fingers running along her naked flesh.

I expect her to be apprehensive or remind me how she's not going to do such things with me, but she surprises me. Sweet little Irina is always surprising me. She sits up on her knees, baring her perky tits to me. Her petite hand curls around my girth, squeezing the base and exploring with her eyes.

"Will it choke me?" she asks, curious and innocent. Her eyes are wide and questioning.

"I hope so." I smirk, tipping her jaw open with the pads

of my fingers. I wrap the tie around her neck and slowly feed my cock into her mouth. She's cautious and timid at first, but I give her an encouraging push with one of my hands tangled in her hair and the other tugging on the tie to tighten it.

She gags a few times, but slurps and sucks like it's a melting ice cream and she's dehydrating. The tip hits the back of her throat and I nearly come.

"You taste so good," she moans, slipping me out and back in.

"I taste of you, dirty girl," I tease, feeling lightheaded and ready to explode.

This girl rocks the entire foundation I've built and stand upon. She makes me lose focus on the world below me because I'm too busy staring straight into the sun. Irina blinds me. Weakens me. Destroys me with her sweetness. And I can't look away. I willingly allow her to ruin every single thing about me.

I'm no longer Vlad, the great Russian mobster who plays the game better than anyone.

I'm hers.

I pull on the tie and feel her throat pinch, squeezing my cock. Her nails dig into my ass cheeks, and I buck into her mouth. Tears build and fall from her eyes, but this magnificent girl doesn't stop. I know she can't breathe. My cock is pushing down her throat, depriving her of air, yet she powers on.

Strong and resilient.

My Shadow, a fiery sun.

Pressure builds in my gut and heat explodes up my spine as my cock throbs. Cum spurts down her throat and fills her stomach. Diana asked me to feed her, and I obliged.

When my cock stops twitching, I slip myself out of her mouth. She gasps for air and tears at the tie to loosen it. She's wheezing and sputtering a little, but then looks up at me with lust and devotion.

"You tasted so good." She licks her lips, and my legs nearly buckle. I've never seen anything so goddamn hot in my life.

Is she even real?

I reach down and yank her to her feet. Cradling her throat, I run kisses along her cheek to her ear.

"Let's shower and get cleaned up. I'm going to need more of you—and soon," I admit, my voice dark and threatening. "You're not leaving this room tonight."

I'm not done with her.

Not by a long shot.

We have *all* night.

Heat encompasses me, and I wake with a start. I haven't slept so good in years. The supple planes of Irina's body are molded to my side, her hair fanned out across my chest. My heart thumps quickly in its cage, and I don't care to free it. Not as long as she's its master.

This is what contentment must feel like.

Warm and comforting.

Lazily gliding through your veins and every nerve ending.

Perfection.

I wish we didn't ever have to leave this room. But we do. Dawn is creeping over the horizon and Diana will return soon. A yawn sounds from Irina as she stretches out her spent body. She's covered in bruises and bite marks. All of which has pride and masculine possessiveness over her surging through me. Of course, they will have to be hidden from her sister. I shouldn't have marked her skin, but I couldn't help myself. I needed to be on her flesh, inside her body, and existing in the very fabric of her being.

I can't let anyone else have her, no matter what Father says.

She's mine.

I've never been more sure of something than I am of this. Fate brought her here, and she will never be far from me. When I'm searching through the dark days, she will light the way and bring me home to her.

We belong together.

I'll do my duty and marry Diana, but the selfish man I am will keep Irina too.

Locked away in my tower like Rapunzel. She will let down her hair for me to climb whenever I choose. And I'll give her a happy ending each time with my tongue.

"You're obsessed with leaving bruises on me," Irina murmurs as she peers into the mirror of my office wall and runs her finger along my newest mark just below her ear.

I lean back in my leather chair and it squeaks. It should annoy me that she waltzes in here any time she wants, but it doesn't. I'm knee-deep in V Games preparation, as well as all the other deeds I'm always responsible for, but I welcome the distraction.

"I think you like them," I taunt.

She glances over her shoulder and bats her lashes at me. "The colors are pretty."

My dick twitches in my slacks. Five minutes ago, I was stressed over the eldest Egorov, a Second Families miscreant who was recently being investigated by the Russian authorities. I'm good at keeping my shit under the radar, but, of all the families, I trust the Egorovs the least when it comes to not blabbing First and Second Families' business. The last thing I need are the authorities up my ass.

But now?

All I can think of is gifting sweet Irina more colorful marks for her to admire.

"Did you wear that dress all for me?" I ask as I tug at the knot of my tie. The room has warmed several degrees now that she's in here. We've been careful to keep our intimate times hidden from others ever since the time we were caught in the kitchen and I had to handle it. I can't afford for any mishaps like that to happen again. Father isn't stupid, and I certainly don't need him sniffing around me right now.

"This old thing?" she teases as she sashays forward. Today she's wearing a black sweater dress that hits above the knee and black leather boots that stop just below the knee. That small view of her knees is enough to drive me mad with the need to turn them bright red with carpet burn.

"Close the door," I bark, my voice husky and rough.

She arches a golden brow and laughs. Goddamn, she's my walking fantasy. Her smiles and laughter are my drug. That body of hers is my sustenance. I crave her with everything in me. "Are we having another meeting?" she sasses.

Meetings.

That's what we tell everyone.

We're having a meeting about the women in the basement. Often, we discuss them and their progress, but mostly, it's an opportunity for me to get her naked and screaming in pleasure.

"Yes," I growl. "Meeting. Now. My desk."

She walks over to my office door and closes it. Her slender fingers flick the lock before she turns back to me. I love what a seductress she is without even trying. So many women have to work for it and sweet Irina was born with it.

"What's the meeting about?" she questions, her eyes flickering with lust.

"Dress code."

She throws her head back and giggles, the sound filling the air around me. My chest expands, and I smile at her.

"You're wearing too many clothes," I complain as I rub at my erection through my slacks.

Her icy blue eyes track my movement and her plump lips painted blood red part. She twists her earring nervously before letting out a sigh. "Fine."

I chuckle and motion with my free hand. "We're waiting."

"We?"

I grab my cock and squeeze. "We."

She rolls her eyes, the nerves leaving her, and begins inching her dress up her thighs. I drink in the creamy flesh as it's revealed until her black silky panties come into view. The material continues to rise slowly, as if she enjoys the art of torture on the side, and her stomach shows. Trim and smooth, but bearing recent hickeys I gifted to her. My cock jolts in my grip.

We like seeing those marks a whole damn lot.

The dress gets tossed away and my gaze falls to her tits

spilling out of her black bra. Irina has the kind of breasts that fit perfectly in the palm of your hand. But this voodoo bra of hers has them looking twice as big. More cleavage. Hot as fuck.

"Leave all that sexy shit on and come here. Boots stay on too," I growl, motioning to the top of my desk in front of me.

She prances my way, comfortable in her own skin. I'd like to think it has something to do with me. When you worship a woman's body, she soon begins to love it too. It shows in her confidence. My sun is finding her way out of the shadows one step at a time.

"I overheard Rada the other day talking to another maid," she murmurs as she sits down in front of me. She lifts her legs, resting both feet on my knees.

"And?"

"She says some women are into choking."

My blood runs cold. "And?"

Irina bites on her bottom lip and her neck turns red. "She told the other girl she's most definitely not into it anymore, but…" she trails off. "I was thinking…"

Don't tempt me, beautiful fucking girl.

Her lashes blink innocently. "Since you like bruises and all…"

"Say it," I bark.

"Maybe you could choke me." Her nostrils flare, but she doesn't cower from her words.

I let out a heavy sigh. "Once you open that door, you can't shut it."

Her brows furl. "I want to open all the doors with you. You started this," she snips. With the toe of her boot, she nudges my hand away from my cock and presses against me.

"So finish it, Vasiliev."

With a growl, I push her knees apart and rise. Her eyes widen at my quick movements, but she doesn't pull away when I grip her throat, gently at first. "Touch your pussy through your panties. Get yourself nice and wet, my sun."

She smiles at me as she rubs against herself with her fingers. And I revel in the way her eyes flutter closed.

Trust.

This sweet young thing trusts me.

An angel giving a devil her wings for safekeeping.

Closing in on her, I inhale her delicious scent. I can smell strawberries from breakfast still on her lips. With a squeeze, I let her feel the power of my grip as I kiss her softly. She half rasps, half moans as her tongue seeks out mine. I kiss her at an unrushed pace as I increase the pressure on my hold. When I hear her sucking air, I pull away.

"You're not scared," I observe as I study her features. Her face has turned bright red and I know if I keep at it, blue will eventually take over as the dominating color. If only she could see the brilliant colors on her face. My sweet Irina would want to paint them. "Watching you gasp for air makes my dick really hard," I admit. "I want to choke you until you pass out only to revive you and do it all over again. Does that frighten you, little Volkov?"

Her eyes flare with strength. I have my answer.

"You truly are perfect," I mutter aloud. I tighten my grasp, and she struggles to keep up the pace as she touches herself. "Don't worry, I'll help you out."

I fumble with my slacks, but soon, I free my cock. I slap at her hand rubbing at her cunt with my rock-hard erection until she pulls it away.

"Let me inside," I order.

She tries to shake her head no, and I can't help the smile that graces my lips.

"I wasn't asking," I warn, tightening my grip.

She grabs her soaked, silky panties and pulls them over her pretty pink cunt to hide her delights from me.

I take a hand away from her throat, but keep the pressure with the one hand. I bat her away from her panties, clutch them in my fist, and tug them until they rip.

Her eyes blaze and I inch inside her until I'm fully seated. The moan that tries to escape her throat is muffled below my grip. I've choked enough women to know just how hard to squeeze without crushing their windpipe. You give them just a sliver of air. Enough to remain coherent but not comfortable. Enough to keep a little fear running through their veins along with the excitement.

Brave Irina stares at me with such trust and desire. She believes I will take care of her and not truly hurt her. I reach between us and finger her clit as I begin thrusting into her tight cunt. My hand compresses tighter. I know I've struck a nerve when she clenches around me. Her legs on either side of me begin to tremble.

Fuck, she's beautiful.

Purple.

So purple.

I thought I preferred blue, but that was because I didn't have this. This was the color I was striving for. The same color as the darkest shade on many of the sunsets she paints. I'll tell her this later so she can appreciate the color as well.

My mouth crushes against hers in a kiss. Her movements are slow and sluggish, already weakened by my death grip on her. I could keep her in this hold, and eventually, she'd pass out. I nearly come at the thought and slam into her so hard, the desk jolts forward.

"That's it," I murmur against her open mouth. I bite at her tongue and pull it out with my teeth, relishing in how dry it already is. Her fat lips are blood red. One day, I'll get her like this right after a shower and under the bright bathroom lights so I can watch her lips turn colors. When I suck her lip into my mouth, her cunt clenches around me again. I'm unravelling. Close. So close. But I want her to lose her mind first. We'll go crazy together.

Her hands lift and I imagine she'll swat me away. Instead, her fingers thread into my slicked back hair and she tangles her fingers in it, messing it up. With surprising strength, she pulls me back to her mouth, desperate for another suffocating kiss. I mold my mouth to hers and kiss her hard, without letting up for a second. Her body trembles and her head lolls back, breaking our connection.

I pound into her, intensifying my efforts on her clit, admiring her perfect purple face.

"Irina!" I bark, jerking her from her daze.

She blinks her eyes open—eyes now turning bloodshot—and stares straight into my motherfucking soul. I let her in. Goddammit, do I ever let her in. Tears leak from the corners of her eyes, and she violently shudders before me. Her cunt clenches hard around my cock and her juices become thicker as she gives into a silent, yet powerful orgasm.

"My beautiful girl," I hiss as I come. My heat explodes out of me, coating her insides. As soon as her trembling slows, I release her throat and pull her against my chest. I wrap an arm around her waist and pull her with me as I sit down in my chair. "Look how perfect you are," I whisper as I kiss her full tits and collarbone.

Her fingers slide back into my hair and tighten. She

yanks until I'm looking up at her. My cum leaks out of her, soaking my slacks, but I don't even care. What we just did was so fucking hot, I want to do it more. A whole lot more.

"I liked that," she rasps, her voice barely audible. A smile tugs at her swollen lips.

Leaning forward, I nip at her chin. "You like being choked?"

Her eyes shine with adoration. "I like the look you give me when you choke me."

"And what look is that?"

She shrugs her shoulders. "I'll have to show you one day. I'll paint it."

"Make sure you add one of those purple sunsets behind me," I say with a grin.

"I would consider that an odd request, but since I just told you I wanted to paint your face while you're choking me, I suppose it's not so odd in the grand scheme of things."

I hug her to me and stroke her hair. "Not odd at—"

Bang! Bang! Bang!

"We're having a meeting!" we both yell out in unison.

CHAPTER SEVENTEEN

Irina

One month later...

The past four weeks have passed so fast. I'm completely addicted to a man who isn't mine.

He's always been yours.

Confusing thoughts surge through my mind, and I try to make sense of them. Some days, I want to convince myself that what Vlad and I are doing is okay. That we deserve this. Other days, I can barely meet my sister's gaze. Guilt consumes me. The only thing not driving me off the edge is the fact that I know she is in love with Ven. Vlad is just another business deal.

She's even faltered a few times while pacing her room, telling me she can't go through with it. Then, in the next breath, she's talking about what's best for us now—her duty. He's just a means to a more influential name to her, but to me...

He's everything.

My waking thought and the one I close my eyes to.

His eyes follow me wherever I go, and I steal glances of the handsome man who knows my body better than I know my own.

Diana has been discussing Volkov Spirits with Father

and Vas, but all I want to do is drown myself in Vlad's intoxicating scent. Wrap my legs around his slim waist and ride him like a prized stallion. He's under my skin, burrowed so deep, I don't think I'll ever get him out.

"So, Vas will be here tonight. I want you to be on guard," Diana tells me, curling the last lock of my hair into a loose ringlet. "He's a slippery one, I just know it." Gathering my hair, she pulls the curls into a fancy up-do, letting a few strands tumble down to frame my face. She strokes a finger down the back of my neck and smiles at me in the mirror. "You have such an elegant neck, Irina. It's just like Mother's."

I replicate her smile and stroke a hand down my dress. It's a daring red, to snare a bull, and I love it. Diana brought it back with her from her trip with Vika.

She steps in front of me and paints my lips the same crimson color as the fabric. "Father is also coming tonight," she tells me, wincing slightly.

"Are you ready?" Diana asks, holding out her hand for me to take.

"Yes."

The music hums through the corridors as we make our way to the great room. People mingle, glasses clink, and heels click-clack over the wood floors. There's a sweet fragrance from the flower arrangements laid out everywhere. "Isn't this supposed to be an eighteenth birthday party?" I mock-whisper to Diana, who grins and squeezes my arm tighter.

"And an engagement party. Vlad told me they will announce Ruslan and Vika's wedding date tonight," she divulges. My heart drops. It's ludicrous and irrational to hate the fact that Diana has been speaking with Vlad in private, but the jealousy followed by guilt slams into me all the same.

She may have conversations with him, but it's my bed he's been coming to nearly every night for the past month.

"Oh, look, there's Ven," Diana sings. I tug on her arm to stop her departure. She turns to face me and furrows her brow. "What's wrong?"

"You can't keep flaunting your affair like this," I hiss, furious that she doesn't seem to care any longer. "It's not as discreet as you may think, Diana."

All the color drains from her cheeks. "Who knows?" she breathes, looking around the room. Tears build in her eyes, so I take her hands in mine and give them a reassuring squeeze.

"No one knows yet. But the way you and Ven flirt, people will start to notice," I explain, low and urgent. She looks perplexed for a moment, then begins to laugh. It's light and airy. Real.

"Oh, God, Irina," she says through her giggles. "Ven and I are just friends."

I raise a neatly plucked brow. "He's not your lover?"

"No, of course not," she assures me, her smile falling. Her heavily painted lashes bat quickly against her cheeks as if she's wondering how I even came to this conclusion. "He doesn't see me that way."

She's crazy. Every man sees her that way.

"Then who?" I ask, dumbfounded. I was sure it was Veniamin.

"Diana, Irina, you're both a vision." Vas's voice wraps itself around us, followed by his arms. He kisses both of us on the cheek, and I want to tell him to jump off a bridge, but the fact is, it's not his fault who his father is. He's our brother. We have a brother.

"Where's Father?" Diana asks, looking around like

there's a bomb about to go off.

"He wasn't feeling well, so I'm here in his place to represent our family in wishing the happy couple luck."

"Ha. He's going to need it," I snort. Poor Ruslan. What a nightmare that has been dropped in his lap.

"Oh, I don't know," Vas croons, dragging his eyes up Vika's body. Yuck.

"She's Medusa, Vas," Diana grumbles. "Look hard enough and you'll turn to stone."

He smirks at Diana's warning. "Well, a part of me certainly has."

I crinkle my nose in distaste. "Gross." Diana cringes. Vas laughs heartily and loud, gaining attention from other party dwellers.

"I'm going to get a drink," I tell them and leave them to find a server. I feel the eyes of many men on me, watching as I pass by them, and nerves form in my stomach. I venture toward the back of the room and slip out of the French doors to grab some air. I've never been good in these environments, and I'm not used to being so on display and noticed. Diana is usually the fantasy on people's minds and the compliment on their tongue, but there's been a shift inside me, and it's visible on the outside to others.

I'm coming out of the shadows and people are noticing.

The door opens behind me, and I shiver from the cold. A sigh of relieved breath escapes me when I see Vlad joining me in the night air.

"I saw you slip out here. It's freezing, Irina," he rumbles as he stands directly behind me, his body heat enveloping me. "What are you doing?"

"They're out here," I argue and nod to some party

attendees mingling out in the courtyard. They're smokers respecting the Vasiliev's home by not smoking inside.

"They're not you." He presses his body against my backside, and I relax against him. "You smell divine." His hot breath in my ear causes me to shudder. "You're cold."

It's a statement, not a question.

I answer him anyway. "Yes."

"Then I should warm you up. You'll catch pneumonia out here."

With that, he shimmies my dress up my legs.

"Vlad," I warn, but he doesn't listen. He never does.

I brace my hands on the stone wall separating me from the twenty-foot drop where all the smokers are. His fingers glide beneath the fabric and pull my panties to the side. "Tilt your pelvis, my sun," he urges. I hear his zipper pulling down and him fumbling to free himself. His heavy cock smacks against my ass and wet arousal floods between my legs. I push my hips back to give him access, and he groans, urging my legs apart with his thigh. His cock slides against me again, and then he's inside me. The burn ignites the raging fire within me, and I'm burning, completely aflame. He thrusts forward, and I want to cry out, but bite down on my lips to hush myself. Strong hands grip my hips, using me as he pleases. I snake my hand down and under the fabric of my dress, finding my throbbing clit. I circle my fingers there just like Vlad taught me via many of our indiscretions this month.

"Pinch it, Irina," he demands, and I obey. The stars dance in the sky above me as the music plays from inside the house. I moan out, unable to stop myself. Vlad shoves his fingers in my mouth, and I bite down hard, coming undone.

The orgasm powers into me, weakening my legs and sending tremors through my bones, curling my toes.

Vlad's thrusts increase, and then I feel his seed flood inside me. Once his cock stops throbbing out his release, he pulls out of me and slips my panties back into place, dropping my dress and kissing my neck.

"The moon is beautiful tonight," I say, feeling like I'm dreaming all of this.

"You're the brightest moon, Irina. There's nothing more beautiful than you."

My breath catches and a tear beads at the corner of my eye. I wish our lives weren't so complicated. That we could walk back in there, hand in hand, standing like fierce lions facing our families as a united front. Telling them that our coupling is one we choose and they can go to hell.

"We should get back inside," he grumbles, his tone sounding much how I feel inside. "You'll catch your death."

"Okay," I murmur. "I'll go in first." All the happiness from moments before drain from my body. I pull away from him and start for the doors.

"Irina," he calls out, stopping me.

I turn to see him prowling toward me with fierce determination glinting in his amber eyes. He grasps my face with both palms and tugs me to his lips, crushing me beneath his claiming kiss. His hands slide down my throat and then down to my hips. He wraps me up in an embrace, holding me so tight I can barely catch my breath. He kisses me raw and unhurried.

This moment is ours.

His tongue duels with mine and right then, I know we're going to be together...

I just don't know how.

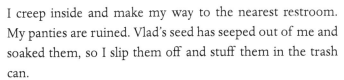

I creep inside and make my way to the nearest restroom. My panties are ruined. Vlad's seed has seeped out of me and soaked them, so I slip them off and stuff them in the trash can.

I wash up and then make my way back to the guests before Diana sends out a search party. I'm just stepping out of the restroom when I hit the steel wall that is Stepan, startling me.

"Hey," I choke out, surprised to see him loitering outside the bathroom. His eyes bore into me as if reading the guilt written all over my sex-heated skin. I try to move past him, but he blocks my way. "Stepan," I say sharply, swallowing down the unease he creates now whenever he is near. "What are you doing?"

He stares at me, his gaze dragging along my features and stalling at my lips. "I dreamed about you." His brows furrow and his eye twitches. I'm a little stunned and don't know what the appropriate response is to that.

"You were sleeping so peacefully in the dream," he murmurs. "So perfect."

My stomach clenches with nerves. "I'm getting a little uncomfortable," I utter, honesty bleeding from my words.

"No," he rushes out, closing in around me. My heart begins to stampede in my chest. "I mean, you don't need to be frightened of me." His tone is urgent. He grips the wall on either side of me, his breath mingling with mine.

"I'm not afraid of you," I lie, trying not to shudder.

"It wasn't a dream though," he says.

"What?"

"I found myself walking past your bedroom," he explains. "You keep your door open at night."

Thud.

"I thought it was a dream," he murmurs and shakes his head trying to clear it. "My thoughts can get chaotic, so I wasn't sure, but that guy was in your room."

Thud.

"What guy?" I'm going to be sick. Is he talking about Vlad? Does he know?

"Your sister's bodyguard. He was watching you sleep."

What?

He's talking about Anton?

"He's harmless," I say, perplexed. "He was probably just checking on me."

He swallows, a look of pure evil passing in his eyes. They're desolate—like I'm looking into a portal to hell itself.

"He was touching himself." He grips my arms and shakes me as if to drive home the point.

What?!

No. No. Anton's like a father to us.

"You're wrong," I choke out, hot tears welling in my eyes as I wriggle in an attempt to leave his grasp.

It's not true.

Stepan is clearly crazy and doesn't know what he saw.

"I'll kill him," he hisses, spittle landing on my face. "For you, I'll kill him." He leans forward and inhales my hair.

I think he's a little insane and confusing weird dreams he's been having with reality.

"Thank you, but I'll deal with this myself."

He releases me, pulling back and pushing into the restroom. I'm left free and completely weirded out. There's a flaw in his code, that's for sure. I rush down the hallway, eager to get away from him. I need to process what he's said to me and far away from him at that.

Vika is in a heated conversation with Ven when I approach a waiter standing close to them. My heart rushes when I see Vlad standing directly behind them. The look on his face turns my blood cold. Violent and furious. It's the face of the killer lying dormant under his skin. Whatever they're discussing, he doesn't like it.

I want to rush over to him and beg him to hold me. Plead for him to tell me everything is fine. That what just happened moments ago was just silly ramblings from a madman. It can't be the truth. My mind won't allow it.

Ven grabs Vika's arm and growls something at her, but Vlad steps back and then takes off. I hurry to follow him and track him to his office. When I reach the doorway, he's already seated, glaring down at his computer monitor. Disgust is painted in an angry sneer on his handsome face.

"Vlad?" I choke out as I rush into his office. "What's wrong?"

CHAPTER EIGHTEEN

Vlad

Her scent is all over me, and it sends my mind racing. I was just inside her, yet I still crave her. She's like a drug I can't cope without. I need a hit constantly.

I search the room for her, but she's nowhere. I made quite a mess of her, so she's more than likely cleaning up. I take a drink from a server and down the contents. Vas-the-new-Volkov approaches, and I haven't had enough to drink to deal with him right now.

"Vlad, or shall I call you brother now?" he asks, a smirk on his face. "You are marrying my sister, after all."

I snort. "You can call me sir or master, Vas."

He narrows his blue eyes on me, and I can imagine the ways he's thinking of carving me up. I'd have the same thoughts if spoken to like that. Running a hand down his cheap suit, he watches the room just like I taught him. "Is that what Diana calls you?" he teases, trying to get under my skin. Foolish boy.

"In fact, it is," I torment. "Or Daddy when the mood strikes."

He grinds his teeth, then makes his first mistake. "Father and I have decided Irina will return home where she belongs. I have plans for her."

Ice cold fury shrouds me in its chilly grip. "She belongs

here, and no one is taking her away," I grit out in warning.

"You get Diana, Vlad," he says. "Irina returns to the fold."

My fist clenches and I'm dying to ram it through his stupid nose like I've done hundreds of times when he answered to me down in the basement. Instead, I glower at him.

"Don't come into my home and make demands of me," I snarl. "It's a death warrant."

"It's not a demand of you," he bites out, ignoring my threat. "It's of her." He places his glass down and saunters off into the crowd.

I'll kill him and feed him to his stupid daddy if he even tries to remove Irina from me.

She's fucking mine.

I spy a server and make my way over to him, stopping when I overhear Vika speaking to Veniamin.

"It's true, Ven, precious Diana and that old man, Anton, are up to no good behind my good brother's back."

"Your lies will get innocent people killed, Vika," Ven grits out. "Diana is nothing like you, so stop projecting." He grabs her arm, sneering down at her.

She snatches her arm and bites back, "I saw them with my own eyes. They were kissing like high schoolers at prom and then disappeared into her hotel room when we went away to buy my dress."

My head begins to throb with information overload. Diana is fucking Anton? He's as old as my goddamn father. Have they been doing that under my roof? Right under my nose for over a fucking month? Is that why she wanted him to come here with her? How did I miss this?

I miss nothing.

Anger explodes within me.

It's not often I get blindsided, and when it happens, I make motherfuckers pay.

I march down to my office, needing answers, and flick the computer on. I bring up the first week's feed from when they arrived in Diana's room and fast forward until my heart stops.

Anton enters her room.

Goddammit.

I knew she wasn't a virgin.

I can't watch that old man rutting on her. I fast forward to him leaving her room and change to the corridor cameras. They must be stupid and have a death wish to do this shit in my house. It's not the fact that Diana is fucking someone else, it's the who, and the deceit—the brazen disloyalty. She told me she was a virgin and insisted on bringing that man here. Leonid will lose his mind over this. If it gets out that I allowed this to happen under my roof with no retribution, I'll be a laughing stock.

I stare numbly at the screen, my mind racing with building anger.

It's been ten minutes that Anton has been back in his own room when his door opens again.

How many times can he go at his age?

But it's not Diana's room he creeps into this time. It's Irina's. My heart feels like it's going to burst from the ribs containing it.

No.

Please fucking no.

If she's sleeping with him too, I'm going to be sick.

My guts coil as I click on the screen to her room.

"Vlad? What's wrong?" Irina's voice calls from the doorway. She floats toward me, and I have to hold up my hand to stop her. If this shows any signs of Anton and her touching, I can't trust myself not to kill her.

I drag my eyes from Irina and glare at the screen. She's asleep in her bed, oblivious to the fact that he's even in there. He stands at the foot of her bed and pulls his cock from his slacks.

Motherfucker.

"Oh, God," Irina cries out. I hadn't even noticed her approach this side of the room.

Her eyes tear up, and she clutches her stomach as if to hold in the sickness she's clearly feeling.

"It was him," she gasps, almost choking.

"What was him?" I demand, my blood igniting with rage.

"I thought it was a dream."

"What, Irina?!" I roar, losing it. I know what she's going to say. I can feel it in my bones. I don't want to hear it, but I need to.

Her eyes are wide and filled with terror like a deer caught in headlights.

"Someone touched me when I was a young girl," she whispers, the tears in her eyes spilling down her cheeks. "Just once, and Diana's presence scared them away. I thought it was a dream, but it's coming back to me. I blocked him out, but now he's so clear. It was Anton."

The rage that had been surging to the surface explodes. I rise to my feet, sending my chair hurtling away from me and grab my monitor. With a furious roar, I launch it across the room and it crashes against the wall. The sound is satisfying, but my fury has no hope of being snuffed out. The calm, collected man has evaporated. In his wake stands the beast—the monster ready to rain hell down on this earth.

Opening a cabinet in the back of the room, I grab my fish hook knife and a bundle of rope.

Someone is going to die.

"Vlad," Irina calls after me. "Vlad!"

I can't listen. I can't stop. I'm going insane. My head is swirling with that motherfucker touching *my* woman, my Irina.

Dirty old man.

My face will be the last thing he sees as I cut him into fucking pieces.

I collide with Diana and Ven as I come out of my office like a tornado. Diana crashes against Ven, and he has to grip onto her to keep her from falling to the floor.

"Vlad?" Diana asks, fear written on her features.

Good, cunt. Be scared. Be so goddamned afraid. This shit ends tonight.

"Where's Anton?" I growl so deadly, she pales and begins to cry.

"Vlad," she pleads, her eyes spilling with tears of betrayal. She knows. She fucking knows what she did, and that I know too.

"Diana," I snap.

She jumps at my tone. "I-I asked him t-to stay in his room t-tonight," she stutters, sobs causing her body to tremble.

I take the stairs three at a time. Irina and Diana give chase, my name on both their lips as they call for me, but I'm faster than them both.

I kick open Anton's door, and he jumps up from the chair he's sitting in.

"What's going on?" he asks, fear flashing in his eyes. He knows. He knows his life ends tonight.

I hit him hard with a closed fist, relishing the crunch of his jaw. His head snaps to the side, and then he's attacking. But I've trained my entire life and easily dodge his punches. With quick moves he can't keep up with, I wrap the rope around his neck, force him into the corridor, and tie the other end of the rope to the railing.

"Vlad!" Diana and Irina cry out in unison.

But it's too late. I'm in a haze of rage, and nothing is dragging me back from it. I flick my knife out, and with enough momentum, I stick it into his groin, digging the blade all the way to the hilt.

"No!" Diana screams as I drag the knife up his stomach, tearing the flesh, cutting an opening right up to his chest. I stand back, then kick him over the railing.

Cries echo around me, and screams resound from below. A loud snap of his neck as it breaks and the splat of his intestines hitting the stone floor cause another ripple of screams.

Diana's fists hit me with surprising force. "No! You monster! Oh God, what have you done?" She sobs hysterically as she beats and claws at me.

"He was an animal," I growl, knocking her hands away from me.

"I love him!" she screams, her sobs broken.

I grab her wrists and drag her to her room. "Loved him. You loved him, Diana. But you can't love him now because he's dead. Now, collect your shit and get the fuck out of my house," I roar. I slam the door, leaving her to pack her things.

Her sobs ricochet off the walls on the other side of the door.

Veniamin has joined Irina, and both are looking down

at Anton swinging. I should have savored that kill, kept him breathing for a few days, relieved him of his putrid cock, then his fingers, hands, tongue.

"Did you hurt her?" Veniamin asks, glancing toward Diana's door.

I can't deal with this bullshit from him too.

"Are you also fucking her?" I bark, shoving him away from me.

He swings a punch, and it hits me in the jaw. My head snaps to the side, and I laugh. It's real and from the gut. I spit out blood and hiss at him. "What a mistake that was, drug." *Friend.*

I ram into him with a shoulder to his chest. We scuffle, slamming into walls and knocking pictures to the floor. A punch to his face, a punch to mine.

"Stop it! Stop it, Vlad, goddamn you!" Irina screams, trying to pry us apart.

Ven manages to force me from him, and I fall straight into Irina. I feel it, the weight of me colliding with her, and her legs giving out. She tumbles back away from me. I reach around to grab her, but hit nothing but air.

The soft thuds as she topples down the stairs stop my heart.

Both Ven and I rush to her aid, but she's at the bottom before we can get to her, landing in the puddle of Anton's blood and guts.

My father and Vas are standing at the bottom of the stairs glaring up at me.

Before I can reach her, Vas scoops Irina up into his arms. She stirs and flutters her eyes at me. Blood coats her skin and soaks her dress. Her eyes are pained.

I can't breathe.

"I'm okay," she mutters, attempting to push from his hold, but she's too weak. "I'm okay." His grip tightens, and he steps away from the bloody mess with my woman in his arms.

I sag, relieved she's not seriously hurt. I start toward her, but Veniamin races down the stairs, knocking past me and out the front door.

Bastard.

My father glowers at me, rage in his eyes. I want to snatch Irina from Vas and run a million miles away from here. I'm about to do just that when a door slams shut and I see Diana with a bag in her arms tearfully eyeing the rope attached to the banister where her dead sicko lover hangs.

I drag my gaze back to Irina, but she's gone.

This isn't over.

This will never be over.

My entire body ripples with fury as I clench the steering wheel. Diana cries silently by my side. I can't even feel sorry for her. My longtime friend royally fucked up. Sure, I was sleeping with her sister, but fucking her bodyguard under my goddamn roof? A man who preyed on her kid sister. Diana was disrespecting me in my own home. Lying to me. But worse, she was letting that bastard stick his cock in her—a cock he seemed much more keen on sticking into her little sister.

"Where are we going?" she murmurs, hugging her bag to her chest.

Ignoring her, I weave through the snow-covered streets.

I didn't even bother with a coat. My anger has heated my flesh to unhealthy degrees. Until I have my Irina back in my arms, I won't calm or settle. I know Father is losing his mind over the scene we caused, but I can't even bring myself to care right now.

All I care about his her.

Sweet Irina.

I need her.

I fucking need her.

"Are you going to kill me?" she asks, swallowing. She lifts her chin bravely and looks my way. I've debated it. But Irina's sorrow would haunt me.

"Nope," I spit out.

She sags. "I'm sorry if I hurt you—"

"You. Did. Not. Hurt. Me." I jerk my head her way and spit out my words. "You made a fucking fool out of me in front of everyone." At least if she were fucking Veniamin, it would have been with a respectable man. I would still need retribution, but Anton? He was nothing more than a servant. An old, dead fucking servant.

She starts to cry again. "Vlad, please…" She swipes her nose with her coat and sniffles. "I'll do whatever I can to make it right. I promise."

"You're done," I hiss out. "I don't ever want to see your face again."

"N-No, I can f-fix this," she chatters, sobs cluttering her throat. She reaches my way and grabs my cock. "We can have sex. I can be a good wife. Please, Vlad. I can fix this. Let me fix this."

I grab her wrist hard enough to have her crying out and jerking it away from me. "I'm fucking your sister."

Her sadness melts away as intense fury overcomes her.

"What? No! I don't believe you."

"She cries so good when I come inside her," I taunt as I pull into the driveway of my location. "I like ruining her for any men. Kind of like how Anton ruined you. You're a whore, and I'll be damned if I'll marry a used-up tramp."

"You and I were friends first," she tries. "Have mercy."

"This *is* mercy, and not for you," I seethe. "It's for Irina."

She bows her head as her shoulders quake with her sobs. "Tell me you're lying about you and her."

"Unlike you, Diana, she was a virgin." I pause and smile evilly at her. "But I use the term lightly because I've fucked her nine ways from Sunday since then."

"Ublyudox." *Bastard.*

She starts rummaging through her bag and pulls out a gun. I'm already out of the car and stalking around the vehicle. Sleet mixed with snow pelts my face, but it does nothing to cool the anger bubbling inside me. I yank her door open and jerk the gun from her. She squeezes out a shot that echoes loudly around us, but I wrench it from her and toss it into the snow. Then I grab her by the hair in one hand and snatch up her bag in the other as I haul her to the massive estate nearly surrounded by thick woods. When I make it to the front door, it opens, and Ruslan stares at me in shock.

"What are you doing here?"

"Where's Yegor?" I roar, pushing past him.

"Please," Diana begs. "Don't bring me here. Vlad."

Her words do nothing to calm me. Instead, I drag her through the dark home until I find Yegor's office. Inside, he sits at his desk, his fat belly out in front of him. Ven stands near him. As soon as Ven sees me, he pulls a gun and points it at me. Vika and Rus enter behind us and sidle up next to Yegor, a show of strength. Laughable.

"What the fuck are you doing?" Ven demands, his glare vicious and evil. It gives me satisfaction to see his eye is turning black and his bottom lip is split.

"You already have one cunt going to wear the Vetrov last name. What's one more? You seem to be pretty into her, Veniamin," I bellow. The control I normally have such a tight leash on is gone. Completely fucking gone.

Ven steps forward, but I stop his movements by shoving Diana hard into him. He catches her and keeps her from hitting the floor. I pull out my hooked knife crusted with Anton's blood and rip apart her bag.

"Oh, how the mighty have fallen," Vika snorts at Diana. The sound of the back of Yegor's hand hitting Vika resonates around the room, and she hits the floor like a stone being dropped into the ocean. Another sign of power. It's weak, and little does he know, I don't give a fuck about Vika. Neither do his sons by the looks of it. Veniamin is too busy eyeballing me and comforting Diana. Pathetic.

"You're a fucking asshole," Ven snaps, hugging Diana to him. She trembles and sobs and it makes me fucking mental with rage.

"Begin training her," I tell Ven icily as I shred everything in her bag. "Father wants a Volkov to prove their name in The Games. I think she's earned that honor." I toss the bag to the floor and pin her with a glare. "Have fun in hell."

CHAPTER NINETEEN

Irina

"**I**'m fine," I say for the tenth time in the last five minutes.

Vas narrows his eyes at me and gives a clipped nod. He's pretty much an asshole, but he was helpful in getting me away from the madness of what happened tonight.

Anton.

Dead.

I'm trying to tap into the feelings that allow me to feel sorry for him, but I can't. He deserved it. He was a predator. But what kills me are the screams of horror that continue to haunt me—screams that came from my sister as she watched the one she loved be brutally murdered in front of everyone.

I shudder, but that makes my sore body ache. The fall down the stairs hurt, and I know I'll be wearing bruises for days, but overall, I'm fine. I just want to change out of this ruined dress and soak in a hot bath.

My mind keeps drifting to the look on his face.

Amber eyes blazing with hate.

I close my own to try to focus on them. He was angry for me. Killed Anton for me. I know it with every ounce of my being. He wanted revenge. To slaughter the man who hurt me. Despite all the fighting and death this evening, a small inkling of warmth provides me comfort.

Tomorrow, I'll check on Diana, and then I'll go to him.

"You're staying here now," Father says, as if reading my thoughts, as he enters his office where Vas and I have been waiting. I jerk my head up and pop my eyes open. My neck aches in protest. He tucks his cell phone into his pocket.

"W-What?"

"Diana has made a mockery of our name, and I will not put my other daughter at risk. I need to clean up this mess."

Sitting across from me, he gives me a smug smile, then pushes the ledger across the table. "Besides, you have work to do here. Work that doesn't seem to get done the correct way in your absence."

Vas stiffens from beside me. For a moment, I feel sorry for him. Father's love is fleeting, and Vas will soon learn that. I hope he enjoyed his time in the limelight because now he'll spend the rest of his life not being good enough for Leonid Volkov. None of his children ever are.

I start to reach for the ledger, but wince in pain. Vas reaches past me and grabs it. He settles it in my lap before sitting rigidly next to me, his focus on me.

"I can help you with the books, but tomorrow, I want to go home," I tell my father, my voice slightly cracking. It's not often I stand up to him.

He sneers. "Don't be foolish, child. You're never going back there. I'll send Vas for your things, but you are home now. Safe. And you'll do as you're told until I can arrange for your marriage to Artur Voskoboynikov."

"I'm not marrying him!" I screech.

"Irina," Vas utters beside me as he touches my knee.

I swat him away. "No, I am not like Diana. I will not be forced into marriage with someone I don't love."

Father laughs, and it's cruel and mocking. "Love? You're a Volkov, dear. We don't love. We do business, and we're good at it. You, child, are a pawn in this and you'll do your part. You'll all do your parts."

"You promised us," I choke out, my tone accusing. "You promised us both that we were just as good as the men of our world. That we can rule the empire and marry whom we chose."

He slams his palm on his desk. "Enough. Your mother filled your head with that nonsense, not me. You will marry who I determine benefits us the most."

"No—" I start again, but Father waves me off.

"You'll do as your told," he snarls.

"I need to go check on Diana," I bite out as I stand. I'm still weak and dizzy, and the room spins. Vas rises and wraps an arm around me to keep me from crashing to the floor. He may be an asshole, but right now, he's the best asshole in the room.

"Diana is safe," Father says. "I just got off the phone with Yegor Vetrov. She is to stay there for the time being. Hopefully, she'll be able to use her charms on one of the Vetrov men and redeem the shame she's brought upon us all." He scowls at me. "The eldest has always been sought after. Not even little Vika Vasiliev could land Veniamin. But your sister will try if she values her family reputation. She owes us a debt. And now the Vasilievs will want retribution. We need to strengthen our name with that of our allies. Then we can finally squeeze out the Vasilievs. We'll become the most powerful family with Vas running the front here, Diana marrying Veniamin, and you marrying Artur."

"I'm not going to marry Artur!" I cry out, my knees buckling.

Vas hugs me to him and breathes against my hair. "Shut up, Irina. Just let it go for now."

I squirm against him, but I'm too weak, and Vas is built like a machine. "Please, Father."

"It is done. I'll negotiate with Iosif to see if Ivan will marry you instead. That would be better than Artur, but I cannot make miracles happen. This is the best we can hope for at the time."

A loud crash resounds from somewhere in the house, then several loud gunshots. I scream in horror and Vas drags me to the corner of the office out of the line of fire. He draws a weapon with his free hand and points toward the door. Father already has his piece pointed at the door.

The hairs on my arm stand on end as though a storm is coming. I can feel the charge in the air. The crackle and hum as the entity nears. My heart leaps in my chest, and I try to pull away from Vas.

"Irina," Vas hisses.

A beast enters the room. Wild and untamed. Dark hair hanging in his eyes, his face splattered with blood.

Vlad.

He carries a machine gun and keeps it pointed at my father as his violent eyes search me out. The moment his lock with mine, they flash with relief. I let out a sob and reach a trembling arm in the air.

"Irina, come," Vlad growls, his voice low and deadly. I've never seen him like this. As though he's a demon recently escaped from hell, determined to wreak havoc on the earth.

I start to pull away, but Vas hugs me tighter to him. "No," he snaps back.

"She's not yours," Father snarls to Vlad. "You've sent Diana away, and that's that."

Vlad's eyes flare with fury and the vein in his neck throbs wildly. He's utterly breathtaking. A dark prince come to save his princess in distress. "That's not that," Vlad seethes. "Your whore of a daughter made a fool of the Vasiliev name, Leonid. She can rot in hell for all I care, but that is *not* that."

I wince at his hate for my sister, but my need for him overshadows it for now. "Vlad," I murmur.

"Give her to me. Now," Vlad hisses, his rage barely contained. If they keep pushing, I am afraid my father is going to eat a bunch of bullets.

"You will not come into my home, boy, and—"

Vlad's eyes darken. "Don't test me, old man."

Sensing the impending explosion, Vas pushes me forward toward Vlad. I stumble, and Vlad rushes over to me, collecting me in his free arm. My arms wrap around his solid frame, and I bury my face against his chest.

Warm.

Safe.

Protected.

"You can't just waltz in here and take my daughter!" Father bellows.

Vlad's tone is icy as he spits out his words. "The hell I can't, Volkov." He kisses the top of my head. "You owe me a fucking wife."

He's silent the entire way home, but he's calmed considerably. The moment we got into his car, his fingers laced with mine and he hasn't let go. Everything hurts, and I'm worried about Diana. Father said she was to make advances on Ven.

That has my nerves settling a bit. Ven is her friend, and I don't think he'd hurt her. It's probably the safest place she could be. My thoughts are still jumbled as Vlad pulls up to his estate. He climbs out, then stalks around the car to fetch me. I start to walk, but he doesn't allow it, scooping me into his powerful arms. He's still quaking with fury, and I crave to calm him in any way I can.

"Vlad," I murmur as I stroke the dark hair from his eyes.

He closes them and stops. The snow falls heavily and sticks to his hair and lashes. He's beautiful. A beautiful, furious monster. All mine.

I run my fingers through his hair and angle his head down. My lips brush across his. He presses a hard kiss to my lips, but then pulls away. Anguished amber eyes meet mine.

"I need to clean you up and assess how badly you're hurt," he says, his voice a low, guttural sound in his throat.

"I'm fine," I murmur.

His gaze intensifies. "If you're fine, then I'll clean you up and fuck you until you're not fine."

I smile at him. "I'm sorry."

Dark brows furl together as he regards me. "For what?"

"Sorry that things couldn't be easy from the get-go. Sorry that everything else had to happen to get this."

He leans his forehead against mine. "I'm not sorry. Not even a fucking little bit. I have you now, and nobody will ever take you away from me. Not your father. Not mine. Nobody."

"Take me home then," I whisper.

And he does.

Vlad leans against the bathroom counter as the shower heats up. His bathroom is much nicer than mine. A walk-in shower with four showerheads on the slate-tiled walls. I'm giddy just thinking about how it will feel on my sore body.

Most of the violence has left Vlad's glare, but sparks ignite here and there. I've never seen him fully unleashed until tonight. Knowing, finally, the monster that lives within somehow comforts me rather than scares me. With slow, shaky movements, I remove my dress and let it fall to the floor at my feet. His eyes skim over my body, flickering every time he sees a bruise inflicted from the fall and not his mouth. Once he's done assessing, I remove my bra. My panties are still missing from earlier. I'm bare and all his.

With a satisfied nod, he starts tearing away at his ruined suit. Piece after piece gets tossed to the floor until he's completely naked in front of me. His cock is thick and proud, jutting right at me. I admire the way his muscles ripple along his tattooed chest with each breath he takes. The two-headed imperial eagle. His brother's name is written into the feathers of one bird's neck and his own name is on the other. Viktor and Vlad. Often, over the past month, I've lingered my fingertips over his muscled flesh and wanted to ask questions. One day, when I think he's ready, I'll ask and hope he'll answer.

He prowls my way and slides an arm around my lower back. Lifting me up, he carries me until we're under the hot spray. I let out a moan of joy. It feels good against my battered back. He sets me on my feet and gathers up my hair in his grip, tilting my head back. The water runs through my hair and down my face, smearing my mascara over my cheeks. I know I must look a fright.

Vlad doesn't care.

Vlad sees past the paints and dresses and shadows.

Vlad finds me.

Hot water rivulets run down his face, taking Anton and Ven's blood with it. Under the sprays, we let the night of horrors wash down the drain.

"I've been drawn to you for so long," he admits, his voice husky. "I played Father's games, but I was a selfish boy. I wanted things I wasn't supposed to have." His nose runs along mine. "I wanted you."

"Always?"

"In some capacity or another since the day I met you. When you were a child, I just wanted you to paint me. To make something ugly and destined for destruction to be beautiful. Just once. I wanted to be something beautiful and worthy even if only for a moment. To capture the real me in one instant and lock me there. I wanted to be yours, then and forever. It didn't make sense, but my heart whispered these things to me. Promised I'd have you one day. You'd do more than paint me, you'd paint yourself all over my soul."

I run my fingers through his slick hair and part my lips. "I'm yours," I assure him. "I always watched you. Crushed on you from afar. A beautiful man I had no business wanting. But I did. I wanted you so badly, Vlad."

He groans as his lips crash to mine. His strong hand grabs my bruised ass, and he lifts me. I willingly wrap my legs around him and invite all of him into me. Slippery between us, his cock ruts until it slides in deep. Both of us moan within our kiss, desperately needing this union more than anything else in our lives.

"I'm going to marry you, Irina," he murmurs against my mouth as he rocks against me. "You're going to get off the pill, and I'm going to fill your stomach with my children.

We'll be everything they don't think we can be. A power-ful force. A match strengthened by our family names, but bound by something much deeper."

I kiss him hard. We've always been more. A silent buzz-ing below the surface. Something powerful just waiting to be unleashed and revealed. Vlad and I were meant to be. I know this deep down in my heart. And although the thought of marriage and being a baby machine never ap-pealed to me—with him, I want it all.

He fucks me raw and beautifully in his shower. With the way he makes love to me, I know he's making promises. Vows so palpable, I can feel them running through my veins straight to my heart.

This is us.

We're a unit now and unstoppable.

His father, my father, the entire world...they are just stepping stones. Insignificant and unworthy.

Strong fingers slip between us, and Vlad rubs me in the expert way that has me losing my mind. My clit throbs for him, and he plays it like an instrument. Soon, I'm screaming in ecstasy, and his seed pumps into me, violent and out of control. My pussy clenches around him, trying to milk his very essence from him.

As his cock softens, he pulls away to pepper sweet kisses all over my face until I'm giggling. In a rare, stolen moment of beauty, Vlad smiles at me. Real and breathtaking. All for me. Only for me. My heart races out of my chest.

"I love you," I breathe, my eyes pinning his.

His gaze darkens, and he leans his forehead against mine. "The way I feel for you is far more powerful than love, little shadow."

CHAPTER TWENTY

Vlad

I've avoided every single person in my home. Including Father. We still haven't spoken since I slaughtered Anton just over a week ago, and I'm not ready to talk to him. I'm still too volatile. I need to be cool and collected when we speak.

Today, I will talk to him, and then everything will go on as if Diana and Anton never happened. We still have a wedding to plan. I've just replaced the bride.

"Mmmm," Irina murmurs in her sleep, her palm rubbing across my pectoral muscle.

I stroke my fingers through her hair, a smile tilting my lips up. Having her in my bed every night and waking up with her in my arms has been heaven. A devil like myself doesn't deserve an angel, but I have one anyway. And I'm never letting her go.

"Good morning," she says, her voice raspy with sleep. She sits up on her elbow and gives me a pretty smile. The sun shines in from the window, causing her blonde locks to light up. I never get tired of looking at her. Never. In fact, she's fairly distracting in that sense.

"Morning, beautiful." I lean forward and kiss her plump lips. I'm about to take things further when my phone buzzes from the table. I groan as I grab it up. "What?"

"No way to speak to your father," Father grunts.

"Good morning, Father."

I refrain from snapping at him and relax against the pillows. Irina starts kissing my chest, doing her damnedest to improve my mood. She knows how my father ruins my days.

"The honeymoon is over, son. I know you have the young Volkov stowed away in your room. She's becoming a weakness," he complains.

"Is this why you called?" I ask, irritation edging in my tone.

"Partly," he bites out. "But I have more business to discuss. My office in ten."

"Nope," I retort. "If it's important, just say it now. I'm busy."

The line goes dead for a moment. Irina blinks at me, and when I flash her an encouraging grin, she starts kissing lower down my torso. Her hand grips my erection, and I bite back a groan. My dirty little vixen wraps her lips around my cock, dead set on making me lose my cool while on the phone with my father.

"You'll announce your engagement this evening," he says after a minute. "I suggest you find a ring. I want the marriage over and done within a month's time."

Irina smiles up at me around my cock, her heavy engagement ring catching the sunlight and nearly blinding me. "I can do that," I grunt. He doesn't need to know I stole her away from the estate three days ago, took her into the city, and found her the most expensive ring I could, and then proposed to her in a romantic way as we strolled through the snow on the way to a restaurant. Those moments are just for us. Not for prying eyes or people who use such things against powerful men. Aside from my explosion last week, no one will ever know how utterly obsessed I am with this woman.

No one but her.

"Is that all?" My words come out as a hiss when Irina grips my balls and takes my cock deep in her throat.

"How are the women?"

"Irina has been training them. They'll be ready and perfect," I tell him, grunting. Each evening, Irina and I have gone down to check on the women. I work with Stepan, and she the women. She's smart and teaches them things that could prove useful in The Games. By next winter, those women will be smart, cunning seductresses.

"The other women," Father says.

"They're being delivered today. They will be kept on the edge of sanity and make the perfect allure for our more depraved players. And with Irina working with the others, this may be our best Games yet."

He laughs scornfully. "What does little Irina know about showing them how to take two cocks at once?"

"Not rocket science, Father."

A growl resounds from his end. "Let's make sure their cunts are kept tight. A stitch or two will ensure this."

"Hmmm," is all I reply. My woman is swallowing my cock, so I'm not completely interested in what my father has to say.

"And, Vlad, maybe I should test drive what they've learned so far. I'll want to have my pick of them," he grumbles.

Of course he does.

"Darya getting boring?"

Instead of answering, I hear the slapping of flesh. A

woman's scream resounds on the other end, loud enough that Irina pops off my cock and frowns at me.

"Darya is learning how to take a fist in her cunt. She's fine."

Irina slowly fucks my cock with her hand, but she's no longer interested in sucking it as she tries to listen to our conversation.

"Now, are we done?" I snap at him.

"We'll discuss the rest later. Give my future daughter-in-law my regards."

I hang up on him without saying bye. "Why are you stopping?"

"What was he doing to her?" she demands, ignoring me. Fire glitters in her blue eyes. It's one of the things I love about her. She's a storm beneath her calm exterior. I like unleashing her from time to time.

"Do you really want to know?"

"Yes."

"I could show you," I tease.

Her brows lift, but she doesn't back down from my challenge. "So show me."

I flash her a wolfish grin before I maul her. Her squeals are adorable as I flip her around and pin her to the bed. When I reach for the lube on the table, she eyes me warily. I make a big show of pouring it all over my hand and smearing the lubricant on my fingers. Her eyes are wide as saucers. "Spread your thighs."

"Vlad," she murmurs. "What do you think you're about to do?"

I run the slick knuckle of my middle finger along her slit, increasing pressure against her clit. "Having fun with you," I tease.

Her eyes narrow, but she doesn't tell me no. Even if she did, it's not like I'm very good at hearing that word anyway. I slide one finger, and then two, into her easily. She lets out a moan when I curl them up and stroke them against her g-spot. I love making her purr like a kitten. Her body yields to my command and obeys so beautifully.

"Vlad..."

"Shhh," I say as I push a third finger into her cunt.

Her moan is loud, and her eyes have fluttered closed. I rub my thumb against her clit as I ease my pinky in. Her cunt is too tight for me to push past the knuckles and slide any more of my hand in there. It makes me wonder how poor Darya is faring.

"Please..."

"What is it you're begging for, little shadow?"

"You. I need you."

I slide my fingers out of her and grab my cock with my slick hand. She moans when I tease her opening. With a quick thrust, I drive into her body. I seek out her mouth with mine and kiss her hard. My hips piston against hers, and I fuck her too rough for the morning. But my sweet girl takes it. She matches my stride and rakes her fingernails painfully down my shoulders.

I bite her lip. She bites my tongue.

I fist her hair. She grabs mine.

We're hell-bent on climbing inside each other.

Soon, via marriage, we *will* become one.

And the entire country will fucking quake under our rule.

"Oh God," she cries out, her orgasm stealing over her.

Her tight cunt clenches around me as she comes, sending me right over the edge. I come inside her, and just like every other day this week, I wonder if I'll knock her up. I've become utterly obsessed with filling her with my cum and getting her pregnant. I want her pregnant and wearing my last name. And since she's no longer on the pill and officially engaged to me, those things could be in the near future.

Once my cock grows soft and my semen runs out of her, I lift up to look at her. Her eyes blink lazily at me and she smiles. Her smiles will be the death of me.

Or perhaps the beginning.

All these years, I've played by the rules of my father's games.

But then I took Irina and made her mine. Those rules and those games aren't ones I'm interested in playing.

I have a new game.

And I make the rules.

It's a game where she and I win.

Each and every goddamned time.

One month later...

"Everything okay?" I ask as I walk over to her.

She stares out the window of the honeymoon suite of our hotel and nods. "It's bittersweet, you know?"

I come up behind her and hug her. She still wears a wedding dress, and I my tuxedo. The affair was an intimate one, with only our families present. Diana didn't come. It was passed on via Veniamin Vetrov to Irina that she had other commitments to attend to. But what sweet Irina doesn't know is I forbade it. Her older sister isn't welcome in my home ever again. Leonid walked Irina down the aisle, and despite their issues, gave his blessing for me to wed her. A Vasiliev marrying a Volkov was always the plan. There may have been some strife between the two families, but in the end, tradition and power won out.

"I'm sorry. She would have made it if she could," I offer, squeezing her to me.

She turns in my arms and lifts a brow. "I'm not stupid, Vlad. She wasn't allowed to come. Let's not start this marriage off with lies."

She misses nothing.

I should know better.

Shame, an unusual and foreign feeling, trickles through me. Am I such an asshole I couldn't allow her this one thing?

I am, unfortunately.

I'll make it up to her, but it was something I simply wouldn't renege on.

"Hey," she murmurs, her palms covering my cheeks. "I understand *why* she wasn't allowed to come. But it doesn't change the fact that it hurt not having my big sister see me on my big day." Tears glisten in her crystal blue orbs. "I'm happy, though. So very happy with you. I want to do this right. Not like our parents. We're better than them. Smarter and stronger. You and I, Vasiliev. It's you and I against our world."

I relax and lean forward to kiss her forehead. "I'm lucky to have you."

"Damn right," she sasses.

Laughing, I pull away and regard my beautiful wife. The word feels strange on my tongue. Most men in our world seem bothered by having a wife, preferring mistresses over the ones who carry their children. I can't imagine ever fucking another woman. Not when I have this one. She's everything to me. Gorgeous, fierce, smart as a whip, and best of all: loyal.

It's time.

To hand her the key to me.

I've never fully given myself to another person, but my sun—my Shadow—has earned this right simply by being her.

"Come sit," I tell her as I motion to a sofa in our suite.

She pulls away and sashays in her glittery white dress that is more sparkly than the snow when the sun peeks through and illuminates it. Maybe it's the person wearing the dress. She certainly has a glow I'm unable to ignore. As she sits, I walk over to my messenger bag holding my laptop and some pictures I keep with me. I grab the bag and sit beside her.

Ever the patient one, she remains quiet with her hands clasped on her lap. The two rings that tie her to me sit heavy on her dainty finger. I love how loud and expensive they are, practically screaming at anyone with eyes that she's not only taken, but she's taken by Vlad fucking Vasiliev.

I pull out the pictures first and hand those to her. She flips through them, chuckling at a few, saying "aww" when she comes across baby pictures, and staring a long time at one of my siblings and me when the twins were babies and I a preschooler. It's actually my favorite picture because even though you can't see her in the picture, my mother is holding the twins in her lap. Father, long ago, sliced her head right out of the photo—out of all the photos. But she's still there, and seeing her hands in the picture helps my memories paint the rest of what she looked like.

"These are sweet," she says when she finishes.

I take them from her and set them on the coffee table. "I loved my siblings. Father was a prick, and they didn't have a mother. I looked after them and kept them out of trouble. Vika, as you know, was precocious and ran around terrorizing everyone. But Viktor? He was my little buddy. We did everything together. I loved him so much…love him, rather."

"I'm sorry for your loss," she breathes. "I can't imagine something happening to my sister."

I pull out my laptop and flip it open. In an encrypted file, I open a series of video clips. The first one is of last year's V Games. It shows Niko coming up behind my brother, trying to stab him. Then, Kami, a skilled fighter within The Games stabs Niko, but he remains standing. The clock ticking away ends The Games, and then, moments later, it shows Niko getting crushed by the razor twins—big motherfuckers who wear spikes on their clothes—and dying after the event officially ended. We learned later, after I scoured the video footage, Niko Vetrov was ordered to be killed because of my sister—something the Vetrovs obviously don't know. Vika, Father, Viktor, myself, and now my wife are the only ones who do.

"That's so brutal," Irina murmurs.

Instead of answering, I open video conversation after video conversation of Vika planning with Niko to take out Viktor. She would remind him, over and over again, his love affair with her twin was sick and disgusting. That our fathers would only agree to one outcome—she and Niko married, producing heirs left and right. Even in the videos, I could tell my best friend at the time was torn. He loved Vika, I truly believe that, but he loved Viktor more. Essentially, being that they were twins, it was like he could have the best of both worlds. She somehow convinced him to kill Viktor. Luckily, he failed. And as an insurance policy, she made sure Niko would die to cover up all her tracks so his family would not come after her.

Vika would die before she would let Niko sleep around on their marriage with her twin. By getting Niko out of the picture, she got revenge on Viktor. My sister destroys everything she touches.

Irina gasps and her pretty mouth pops open. "Viktor and Niko?" she breathes.

"You know how that would go down in our world, Irina."

I play a clip of Vika revealing Viktor's bisexuality to our father. Father went ballistic, even going as far as to strike my sister in a fit of rage before destroying everything in his office. There are more clips of her meeting with the razor twins and paying them money. No doubt her insurance policy if Niko didn't do her bidding properly. By the time all the clips have ended, I'm furious all over again.

"So, Vika ordered Niko to kill Viktor, but he failed and was ordered to be killed because of it," she mutters, pointing at the first clip. "But if he failed, how did Viktor die?"

I take her hand and kiss her knuckles. "You take this to your grave, Shadow."

Her blue eyes become as wide as saucers. "He's not dead."

My heart thumps in my chest. Father has planted him right smack dab in the US in a state called Arkansas. Right in the middle of nowhere. Punishment for his spoiled prince. To be a nobody. To have to blend in with normal people.

"He's very much alive," I assure her as I open another folder. Inside is information about my brother's location. "If anything ever happens to me, it is your duty as my wife to make sure he continues to be taken care of."

She nods emphatically. "Without a doubt, Vlad."

"Diana can never know this. I know you love her, but nobody knows he is okay. Father faked his death for a reason—to force my brother to live in shame and be alone for the rest of his life." A growl rumbles through me, hate for my father and Vika brimming to the surface. "But mark my words, Irina, I will bring him back home to me one day. I'll find a way. I'll watch and plot and play this fucking game. And one day, when the time is right..." I trail off.

"You'll go get your brother," she replies, her blue eyes flaring with ferocity.

"Damn right I will."

She smiles as she plucks the laptop from my grip and sets it on the table. Then, she straddles my lap with her poufy dress smashed between us. Her brows furrow and an evil glint dances in her gaze. "And Vika?"

"V is for vengeance," I mutter. "V is for Vetrov."

She laughs and kisses me quickly. "What did poor Ruslan Vetrov ever do to you to deserve *that*?"

"Not my problem."

"Someone ought to send *her* into The Games," she grumbles. "She's horrid. I hate her for what she's done to your heart."

That makes two of us.

"With Yegor as a father-in-law, I imagine every day is like The Games with her. Yegor is known for backhanding a viper for talking back. And that's all Vika knows how to do. Assuredly, her life is hell there, especially now that she has been wed to Ruslan. That kid is a prick like his dad."

"Good." Her nostrils flare.

Neither of us speak about the fact that Diana will have

the same fate. But unlike my sister, Diana is a much better player. Landing with the Vetrovs, assumedly Ven, unless Yegor decides otherwise, was her best possible outcome. The alternative would have been meeting the same fate as Anton.

Diana was given a pardon because I love her sister.

"These games," Irina says, frowning. "We're always playing them."

I tangle my fingers in her hair and draw her to my mouth. Running my tongue along her pouty bottom lip, I relish in the harsh intake of her breath. "But now we play for the same team."

"The best team," she agrees, her hands sliding to my shoulders.

I growl, "The *only* team."

We kiss hard and deep, sealing yet another vow.

Irina and I are an unstoppable pair.

Vile.

Vicious.

Villainous.

Vasiliev.

CHAPTER TWENTY-ONE

Vlad

Five months later…

We've been married for five months, yet it still feels like yesterday. The honeymoon period my father assured me would fizzle out within weeks of being a husband, is, in fact, still in full swing. My father has never loved a woman the way I do Irina. If he had, he would have never allowed her to escape his clutches.

I turn toward her and rub a hand over her ass, which is fuller than it used to be. She likes her food, and I like the new curves it's given her body. I could sail the waves of her body forever and never get sick. She's my light—she illuminates my sky. My world. When we're together, sparks fly, igniting us both, and no one could dull our shine.

"I love how round your rump is these days, solntce moyo," I tell her before biting into it like it's a peach.

She giggles and swats me off her. "My clothes have gotten a little snug."

"You like your food," I tease.

"I'm carrying your child."

Her words dance around in my mind, but I can't quite grasp them. "My child?" I utter, searching her face for truth. "Irina."

She bites her lip, her eyes dancing with love. This must be what true happiness feels like.

"Say it again," I command.

She rolls her eyes, and shouts, "I'm pregnant!"

"You're pregnant," I burst out, joy beaming from me. I turn her body so she's now on her back and rest my hands over her slightly thicker stomach—something I hadn't noticed until now. The stomach with my seed inside growing and flourishing.

"Thank you," I murmur. It's the most vulnerable I've ever allowed myself to be in front of anyone and I mean those two words. She brought back parts of me I thought I'd lost. She recovered me from the depths of darkness—the grief of losing my brother. She shone her light on me and warmed my frozen heart. I climb her body and kiss her lips. "I love you," I reveal with a growl.

And then I show her just how much.

I check my watch and wonder if two hours is enough time for Irina to recover from our thorough lovemaking this morning. Based on how she conked out immediately after, completely spent, I figure she could use another hour. She's growing my child after all, and has been for the past three months, she later divulged.

Leaving my office, I see Stepan at the bottom of the stairs, his hands resting on Irina's shoulders as she drops her eyes to the floor.

What the ever-loving hell?

He removes his hands when he sees me approach, and

Irina swipes at a tear falling from her cheek. My protective instincts have me reaching out and grasping him by the neck, crashing his back into the wall.

"Vlad!" Irina screeches, tugging on my arm.

I don't think so, sweet girl.

"You have two seconds to tell me why your hands were on my wife," I growl, spittle spraying his face.

He doesn't flinch or fight me. He knows better.

"I was just asking him to protect Diana in The Games," Irina cries, exasperated.

I grit my teeth, then release Stepan. He rolls his head over his thick shoulders and straightens his shirt.

Ah, yes, The V Games.

The Games are fast approaching, and the humming of anticipation is rife. Diana is to enter The Games in just three short months. I'd thrown out my wishes, not fully expecting anyone to listen. However, a change has been made recently by Yegor and Leonid. I didn't think Ven would allow her to enter, but something has happened we're not privy to.

Yet.

I will find out.

I know everything, and I will know about this too.

I didn't send a viper into their household just to punish her. Vika is useful for information. A cunning little snake.

"You come to *me* in the future, solntce moyo. Now, go eat. You are eating for two now." I kiss her on the top of the head.

"I'm sorry, Vlad. She's my sister."

"And I'm your husband. Your heart and who it loves are mine to protect. I will always protect you."

She sniffles and strokes a hand over my cheek. "I love you," she whispers. I take comfort in her touch and mourn it when she pulls back. I watch her retreating form as she goes up the stairs and disappears from sight.

Turning my attention back to Stepan, I follow his gaze as he traces Irina's steps with his eyes.

"She's pregnant?" He sounds defeated.

"Is that your business?" I snarl. Watching him, his eyes have lingered on Irina too long, too many times. I close in on him. "You'll represent me in The Games, honoring the Vasiliev's ability to train real warriors. Diana made her own fate."

A crease forms on his forehead. "What about what Irina asked of me?"

I once again grab his throat and squeeze. "Is Irina your master?"

It takes an extra squeeze, but then his eyes water without his permission, the rage I've been coaxing into him brimming. "No, sir, you're my master," he chokes out.

"That's right. I am." I release him and lean into his ear. "Who is your target in The Games?"

"Artur Voskoboynikov," he answers, and I smile.

"Good."

Very good.

I seek Irina out and find her in her studio. I know it's crazy, but when I haven't seen her for a while, I miss her. Her lips, her scent, her words, her pretty little pussy. If she's not perched in the chair across from my desk each day tapping away on her laptop as she crunches numbers for not only Volkov Spirits, but for all of my accounts, she's painting in her studio. The numbers make her feel useful, but the painting makes her smile. She's so happy, which makes me really fucking happy.

"Hello, my beautiful wife," I greet with a grin. "I brought you some lunch." I enter her space and place the sandwich I had Rada make down. As soon as the Volkov women entered my home many months ago, Rada backed off and stopped trying to get my attention. Now she just does her fucking job like she's paid to do.

"I have something to show you," she beams, paint dots giving her colored freckles.

"Oh?" I question, creeping across the floor and scooping her into my arms. Her lips are soft and warm, and my dick hardens when her wet tongue snakes out to tease mine.

"You captivated me, Vlad, since I was a young girl. To me, you burn brighter than any sun, and there's no place I'd rather be than here in your arms. Wearing your ring. Carrying your child. When I watch you, it's a perfect view. You're my muse," she breathes, pulling away from me. She picks up a canvas, turning it and placing it on a stand.

My eyes track over the image staring back at me. It's me. The sun lighting my face. There are colors inside me I've never seen before all captured in the version of me she must see. The brush strokes are delicate and precise. There's a smile on my lips as I peek up through my lashes. It's the expression I must have when I'm looking at her before devouring her.

It's the me I always want to be.

"It's beautiful, solntce moyo."

"You're beautiful, moye luna."

EPILOGUE

Diana

The V Games...

So much has happened in a year.

My sister, I have learned through the Vetrovs, is swollen with Vlad's child. A niece or a nephew. Part spawn of the devil and part angel. But still, half my sweet sister. Sorrow washes over me for all I have lost—the biggest loss being her.

How did I even end up here?

Hate surges through me like a monsoon.

Men.

Men are the reason.

Bad men.

Entitled fucking men who think they can do whatever the hell they want.

I lost everything because of men. Stripped of my power, my company, my dignity, my sister—my life.

They think I will die in The Games. I know it, and partly, I think my father would prefer it. Wipe the slate clean like the Vasiliev family did with poor Viktor. Those motherfuckers have another thing coming.

They will not end me.

I pat the hilt of a knife my sister had sent to me that's

tucked into the waistband of my pants under my shirt. It came wrapped under the guise of a pretty dress, a recent picture of my very pregnant sister, along with some scarves. My sister, although living with the enemy, has not forgotten me. She sent me the very item used to kill Anton. It's been cleaned and sharpened, but I will use it to gut the monsters in The Games.

I will kill them all.

Well, all but one…

Living under the same roof as Vika has proven useful. She snaps and reveals truths in anger. Her tongue is like a pot of gold for someone collecting ammunition against the First Families.

They will all know my wrath.

Everyone who has ever crossed me will taste the steel of my blade.

"You don't need to do this," Irina says, grabbing my hand. I'm dragged from my hate-filled thirsty thoughts and regard my sister. I haven't seen her since Vlad so crudely ripped me from his home and dropped me into that of another.

She's beautiful.

Mature and elegant.

A queen in our world.

I'm torn between wishing her all the happiness and hoping her horrible husband dies a thousand deaths, leaving her and their child alone. Guilt, because I do still love my sister, prevails. I want her to be happy. She, of all people, deserves it.

"Let me talk to Vlad," she whispers, squeezing my hand. "Or Father. Maybe Veniamin. I'll talk to them all."

But it's too late.

I'm here. It's already been decided.

I will fight to the death in The Games.

If she only knew Vlad put this in motion many months ago and Father agreed to it.

Pain ripples in my chest.

For *him*.

Not Vlad.

Veniamin.

I didn't mean for things to turn out this way. I never meant to break him so badly.

But I did.

And this is my punishment.

I'm not referring to The Games, but to the crushing ache in my chest. The squeezing of my heart and deflation of my soul.

I broke him.

I broke me.

I broke us.

With a sad sigh, I stroke my fingers down Irina's silky hair before pulling her to me and holding her tight. I love her so much, but my mind is a mess. My little shadow crept out from behind me and took everything that was supposed to be mine.

I don't hate her for it. I couldn't hate her ever. These actions led me to where my soul truly belonged.

To him.

To Veniamin.

If things hadn't turned out the way they did, I would have never known real love and devotion that past few months. What I had with Anton was different. Confusing and wrong. It's taken months and months of reflection to realize that. Anton came to me when I was just sixteen. Did things no man my father's age should have done to a teen. I didn't speak of it. Simply let him use my body because he swore he loved me and we were meant to be. I was such a stupid, stupid girl and fell for every manipulative word.

Ven, when I came to live with them, opened my eyes and helped me see. Made me realize the monster that was Anton. For a moment in time, I thought I'd finally found happiness. And then it all went to shit.

Glancing over my sister's head as we hug, I search the room for Ven, but he isn't here. He couldn't even face me. Not even to say goodbye. I certainly don't blame him.

"Diana," Vas greets.

Irina pulls away as Vas tugs me into his arms. I allow it, but don't hug him in return.

"Father asked me to give you this." He hands me the family blade, our crest emblazoned on the hilt. "Bring his name honor," he tells me.

I clutch the weapon by the blade, closing my palm around it and relishing the sting as it cuts into me. Irina gasps and steps back when my blood drips on her shoe.

I smack the weapon against Vas's chest and sneer. "That's the only blood I'll be bleeding for this family. I'll conquer The Games for me, no one else. He has no honor."

"Diana," Irina breathes, but I'm not the sister she once knew. I've been hardened by grief and heartbreak.

"Irina, come," Vlad calls, summoning my sister. His voice is colder and harder than I remember. I don't recoil though. I'm colder and harder too.

Our eyes clash briefly, but the rage I once saw in them has dissipated with time. My betrayal rendered me trash, yet him doing the same thing with my sister got him a wife and Volkov Spirits. It awarded him a child growing inside

Irina's stomach.

I smirk in his direction, unafraid.

I won't spill tears or blood for lost opportunities. He isn't worthy of my revenge. I have my vengeance set on the man who stole life from me.

Yegor Vetrov.

I move toward the weapons trunk and take out my favorite pieces. The clock sounds to the right of me, and the rail goes up behind me, separating me from the rest of the people in the room.

Irina calls out to me, "Ya lyublyu tebya." *I love you.*

"Good luck," Vas says and nods.

I smear the blood from my palm over my shirt and grin. I'm going to win The Games. Win my freedom and come for the empire that is rightfully mine.

You will all reap what you sow.

And then there will be a new master in this fucked up world. Every *man* will learn to bow at my feet. I will rule them all.

The end for now...

Read the next thrilling story in book two of The V Games

Volcanic.
Victorious.
Valiant.
Vetrov.

PLAYLIST

Listen on Spotify

"Change (In the House of Flies)" by Deftones

"War of Hearts" by Ruelle

"Sucker for Pain" by Lil Wayne, Wiz Khalifa, Imagine Dragons

"Dark Side" by Bishop Briggs

"Killing in the Name" by Rage Against the Machine

"Bullet With Butterfly Wings" by The Smashing Pumpkins

"Cupid Carries a Gun" by Marilyn Manson

"Cumbersome" by Seven Mary Three

"The Morning After" by Meg Myers

"Alive" by Pearl Jam

"Heathens" by Twenty One Pilots

"Monster" by Meg Myers

"Run, Run, Run" by Tokio Hotel

"Everybody Wants to Rule the World" by Lorde

"Dark Nights" by Dorothy

"Going to Hell" by The Pretty Reckless

"Devil Side" by Foxes

"I Put a Spell on You" by Annie Lennox

"Terrible Lie" by Nine Inch Nails

"What's Your Fantasy (Featuring Shawna)" by Ludacris

"The Red" by Chevelle

"Heart Heart Head" by Meg Myers

"Black" by Pearl Jam

"Every Breath You Take" by The Police

"What's Up?" by 4 Non Blondes

"Oh My" by Big Wreck

"Uninvited" by Alanis Morissette

"Deficiency" by Bad Pony

"Testosterone" by Bush

ACKNOWLEDGEMENTS
from KER DUKEY

Thank you to you the reader for joining us on yet another thrilling ride. Your passion and excitement make writing these co-written titles with Kristi an absolute pleasure.

Kristi, thanks for being hard working, and eager to jump back into the dark, beautiful world that we created. You've been amazing to work with as usual and I believe we push each other to be better writers.

You're not just a co-writer, you've become a valued friend. Love you, Lady.

My family always sacrifice time with me so I can work on creating book babies, thank you for being patient, eating takeout when I'm too tired to cook for you. For wearing creased clothes because Ironing is a waste of life hours and for putting up with me wearing headphones for 80% of the day and making you repeat what you tell me at least three times before I listen.

These titles don't happen with just us so **THANK YOU** to all the below:

Editor: Monica, thanks for joining us for another thrilling journey, we value your advice and your awesome skills.

Formatter: Stacey, you know we love you and your mad

skills. This title wouldn't be complete without your pretty touches. Thank you for always making space for us.

Betas: Thank you for your early input and excitement that keeps our mojo high.

A huge thank you to Liana Vanoyan for translating our Russian!

Proof/Arc readers: Thanks to Rosa, Teresa, Nicky, and Allison, for any little typos you caught and your feedback.

Bloggers. We adore you for all your passion, time and help with sharing, reading and getting our work out there.

Indiesage PR: Thank you for all your hard work with release and promo packets. You guys rock.

Authors/friends: Thank you for sharing and caring. For letting us nip in your groups and for offering advice when asked. You are our unicorns. I'm not going to add names incase I miss someone and they put their voodoo on me for it :p

My group: (Dukey's darker souls) Thank you to my wonderful admin and incredible readers, cheerleaders, nosey parkers and slutty members. I love you guys so hard and look forward to chatting with you guys daily. I can share anything with you all and you're supportive and open. I'm so lucky to have such a fierce bunch of ladies having my back. Thank you.

PA: Terrie, thank you for always having my back and being there to pick up the slack if I need to take a moment. You've always been my friend before my PA and I love you.

Kirsty Moseley,
I love you hoe bag. I would be lost without you. Thanks for being an incredible friend to me. We live on opposite sides of the country and see each other once or twice a year if we're lucky, yet we speak everyday, you're one of my best friends and I love you.

ACKNOWLEDGEMENTS
from K WEBSTER

A huge thanks to my co-writer, Ker Dukey. We always have such a blast writing together and I enjoy every moment of it. I hope we can continue to create evil love stories for years to come. You're my boo and I love you!

Thank you to my husband. You're my rock. Always. I love you.

A huge thank you to my Krazy for K Webster's Books reader group. You all are insanely supportive and I can't thank you enough.

A gigantic thank you to my betas who read this story. Elizabeth Clinton and Misty Walker. You all helped make this story even better. Your feedback and early reading is important to this entire process and I can't thank you enough.

Thank you so much, Liana Vanoyan, for being our Russian translator!

A giant thank you to Misty Walker for reading this story along the way and encouraging me!

Thank you to Jillian Ruize and Gina Behrends, for proofreading this book and being such supportive friends. You ladies rock and I adore you all!

A big thank you to my author friends who have given me your friendship and your support. You have no idea how much that means to me.

Thank you to all of my blogger friends both big and small that go above and beyond to always share my stuff. You all rock! #AllBlogsMatter

Monica with WordNerd Editing, thank you SO much for editing this book. You're a rock star and I can't thank you enough! Love you!

Thank you Stacey Blake for being amazing as always when formatting my books and in general. I love you! I love you! I love you!

A big thanks to my PR gal, Nicole Blanchard. You are fabulous at what you do and keep me on track!

Lastly but certainly not least of all, thank you to all of the wonderful readers out there who are willing to hear my story and enjoy my characters like I do. It means the world to me!

ABOUT
KER DUKEY

My books all tend to be darker romance, edge of your seat, angst-filled reads. My advice to my readers when starting one of my titles… prepare for the unexpected.

I have always had a passion for storytelling, whether it be through lyrics or bedtime stories with my sisters growing up.

My mom would always have a book in her hand when I was young and passed on her love for reading, inspiring me to venture into writing my own. Not all love stories are made from light; some are created in darkness but are just as powerful and worth telling.

When I'm not lost in the world of characters, I love spending time with my family. I'm a mom and that comes first in my life, but when I do get down time, I love attending music concerts or reading events with my younger sister.

News Letter sign up
Amazon author page
Website
Facebook
Twitter

Contact me here
Ker: Kerryduke34@gmail.com
Ker's PA : terriesin@gmail.com

ABOUT
K WEBSTER

K Webster is the *USA Today* bestselling author of over fifty romance books in many different genres including contemporary romance, historical romance, paranormal romance, dark romance, romantic suspense, taboo romance, and erotic romance. When not spending time with her hilarious and handsome husband and two adorable children, she's active on social media connecting with her readers.

Her other passions besides writing include reading and graphic design. K can always be found in front of her computer chasing her next idea and taking action. She looks forward to the day when she will see one of her titles on the big screen.

Join K Webster's newsletter to receive a couple of updates a month on new releases and exclusive content. To join, all you need to do is go here (www.authorkwebster.com).

Facebook:www.facebook.com/authorkwebster

Blog: authorkwebster.wordpress.com

Twitter: twitter.com/KristiWebster

Email: kristi@authorkwebster.com

Goodreads: www.goodreads.com/user/show/10439773-k-webster

Instagram: instagram.com/kristiwebster

BOOKS BY

KER DUKEY

Empathy series

Empathy

Desolate

Vacant

Deadly

The Deception series:

FaCade

Cadence

Beneath Innocence - Novella

The Broken Series:

The Broken

The Broken Parts Of Us

The Broken Tethers That Bind Us—Novella

The Broken Forever—Novella

The Men By Numbers Series

Ten

Six

Drawn to you series

Drawn to you

Lines Drawn

BOOKS BY
K WEBSTER

The Breaking the Rules Series:
Broken (Book 1)
Wrong (Book 2)
Scarred (Book 3)
Mistake (Book 4)
Crushed (Book 5 – a novella)

The Vegas Aces Series:
Rock Country (Book 1)
Rock Heart (Book 2)
Rock Bottom (Book 3)

The Becoming Her Series:
Becoming Lady Thomas (Book 1)
Becoming Countess Dumont (Book 2)
Becoming Mrs. Benedict (Book 3)

War & Peace Series:
This is War, Baby (Book 1) - BANNED
(only sold on K Webster's website)

This is Love, Baby (Book 2)
This Isn't Over, Baby (Book 3)
This Isn't You, Baby (Book 4)
This is Me, Baby (Book 5)
This Isn't Fair, Baby (Book 6)
This is the End, Baby (Book 7 – a novella)

2 Lovers Series:

Text 2 Lovers (Book 1)

Hate 2 Lovers (Book 2)

Thieves 2 Lovers (Book 3)

Alpha & Omega Duet:

Alpha & Omega (Book 1)

Omega & Love (Book 2)

Pretty Little Dolls Series:

Pretty Stolen Dolls (Book 1)

Pretty Lost Dolls (Book 2)

Pretty New Doll (Book 3)

Pretty Broken Dolls (Book 4)

The V Games Series:

Vlad (Book 1)

Taboo Treats:

Bad Bad Bad

Easton

Crybaby

Lawn Boys

Malfeasance

Carina Press Books:

Ex-Rated Attraction

Mr. Blakely

Standalone Novels:

Apartment 2B

Love and Law

Moth to a Flame

Erased

The Road Back to Us

Surviving Harley

Give Me Yesterday

Running Free

Dirty Ugly Toy

Zeke's Eden

Sweet Jayne

Untimely You

Mad Sea

Whispers and the Roars

Schooled by a Senior

B-Sides and Rarities

Blue Hill Blood by Elizabeth Gray

Notice

The Wild – BANNED

(only sold on K Webster's website)

The Day She Cried

My Torin

70657980R00140

Made in the USA
San Bernardino, CA
04 March 2018